THE SCREAM OF
THE HAUNTED MASK

Goosebumps HorrorLand

ALL-NEW! ALL-TERRIFYING!

NOW WITH BONUS FEATURES!

LOOK in the back of the BOOK for exclusive author interviews and more.

NIGHT OF THE LIVING DUMMY

DEEP TROUBLE

MONSTER BLOOD

THE HAUNTED MASK

ONE DAY AT HORRORLAND

THE CURSE OF THE MUMMY'S TOMB

Goosebumps HorrorLand

THE SCREAM OF THE HAUNTED MASK

R.L. STINE

SCHOLASTIC

Scholastic Children's Books
A division of Scholastic Ltd
Euston House, 24 Eversholt Street
London, NW1 1DB, UK
Registered office: Westfield Road, Southam, Warwickshire, CV47 0RA
SCHOLASTIC, GOOSEBUMPS, GOOSEBUMPS HORRORLAND, and
associated logos
are trademarks and/or registered trademarks of Scholastic Inc.

First published in the US in 2008 by Scholastic Inc.
This edition published in the UK by Scholastic Ltd, 2008
Goosebumps series created by Parachute Press, Inc.

ISBN 978 1407 10692 2

British Library Cataloguing-in-Publication Data.
A CIP catalogue record for this book is available from the British Library

Printed in the UK by CPI Bookmarque, Croydon
Papers used by Scholastic Children's Books are made from wood grown in
sustainable forests.

5 7 9 10 8 6

www.scholastic.co.uk/zone

3 RIDES IN 1!

THE SCREAM OF
THE HAUNTED MASK

I clicked on the basement light. Then I gripped the iron banister and took a step down. The stair creaked beneath me. It sounded like a squeaking mouse.

I took another step, squinting into the yellow light. The cold stairs chilled my bare feet. I lifted my long nightshirt so I wouldn't trip over it as I made my way down.

In sleep, my straight brown hair had fallen over my face. I brushed it back over my shoulders. My hand trembled with fear.

I heard a hum in the basement as the furnace clicked on. Another stair squeaked beneath me. I stopped halfway down.

"What am I doing?" Did I say the words out loud – or did I only think them?

Why was I creeping down to the basement in the middle of the night?

It wasn't my idea. I didn't want to do it. I was being pulled ... pulled against my will.

Carly Beth . . . Carly Beth. . .

As if the terrifying mask was calling my name. The ugly Haunted Mask that tried to ruin my life . . . tried to destroy my brain . . . tried to turn me evil.

And now it was calling me. Forcing me down the stairs and across the cold basement floor.

Carly Beth . . . Carly Beth. . .

I knew I wasn't dreaming. My fright was too real. I switched on the ceiling light. It glowed off the bright red vinyl chairs and sofa in our playroom. I grabbed the edge of the ping-pong table. I tried to stop myself. Tried to hold myself back.

But the pull of the mask was too strong.

I suddenly felt so weak and tiny – like a piece of dust caught in a powerful vacuum cleaner. My hands flew off the table. I stumbled forward, my toes tangling in the strands of the white shag rug.

My horse posters . . . the red wall clock . . . my brother Noah's old tricycle . . . the closet door covered with family snapshots . . . all swept by in a blur as I staggered across the basement.

To the storage room against the far wall. To the mountain of cartons and old furniture and piles of baby toys and old clothes and magazines. The room where I had buried the mask. So deep in the stacks and stacks of junk that no one could find it.

And now it was calling me . . . pulling me.

Carly Beth . . . Carly Beth. . .

Was the whisper only inside my head? The sound of *my own name* sent shiver after shiver down the back of my neck.

I knew what it wanted. I knew why it woke me up and called me from my bedroom.

It wanted me to uncover the metal box where I had buried it away. To unlock the box and free it. To pull it on again this year. To let its evil sweep over me once more.

The Haunted Mask was ready to take over my mind again and force me to do its evil.

I couldn't let that happen. I would never let that happen again.

But here I was, stepping into the dark storage room. Squinting at the piles of cartons and old furniture. Here I was, unable to fight it.

My legs trembled as I lifted the first box. Shivering in my thin nightshirt, I pulled the heavy carton off the pile and set it down beside me. Then I reached for the next carton.

"I can't stop myself!" My voice came out in a choked whisper.

I wanted to turn away. I wanted to run. Instead, I bent and pulled the metal box out from its hiding place. An old black box with a heavy clasp. I let out a gasp. The box felt WARM!

What was I *doing*? Why couldn't I stop my hands?

My heart skipped a beat. I made a choking sound as I unlocked the box and lifted the lid.

5

Folded inside the box, the mask let off a green glow. I gaped at the two crooked rows of fangs. The fat, rubbery lips grinned up at me.

"Stop, Carly Beth! Stop! Don't do it!" I pleaded with myself.

But I was no longer in control. I wrapped one hand around the bumpy bald head of the mask and lifted it from the box.

"Ohhhh." A groan escaped my throat. The mask felt like *human flesh*!

The pointed chin bobbed up and down. The rubbery lips made a *bub bub bub* sound as they rubbed together.

I couldn't breathe. My chest felt ready to burst.

I let the box fall to the floor and raised the ugly mask high over my head. The sunken eye holes grew wider. The wormlike lips made their *bub bub bub* sound.

The basement cold wrapped around me. I could feel my muscles tighten. My whole body was stiff with fear.

I began to lower the mask . . . lower it over my head.

I felt the warm rubbery material against my hair. I tugged it down. Soft as human skin, the mask slid over my forehead.

And then . . . "NOOOOOOOO!" A shout burst from my throat.

A scream of fear and anger all mixed together.

6

The force of the shout gave me strength. I pulled the mask up and jerked it away from me.

"NOOOOO! You're not going to overpower me. I'm not going to wear you – ever again!"

I gripped the warty cheeks of the mask in my fists. Then I gasped as the mask moved its rubbery, warm lips. *Bub bub bub.*

The lips parted and the fangs tilted up.

And the Haunted Mask opened its mouth in a long, deafening SCREAM!

The next afternoon, my friend Sabrina Mason followed me on to the bus. We rode it every day to our after-school job.

"Carly Beth, are you OK?" Sabrina asked, swinging her backpack off her shoulders. "You look like something my cat coughed up."

I laughed. "Why don't you say what you *really* think, Sabrina?"

Sabrina and I have been best friends since third grade. So we can almost always say what's on our minds without either of us getting hurt.

We're both twelve. But Sabrina looks at least sixteen. She is tall and dark and graceful and sophisticated looking, with long black hair and enormous black eyes.

I'm stuck with this little pixie face, a tiny stub of a nose, and a skinny mouse body. I'm actually a month older than Sabrina. But people think I'm her younger sister!

The bus started up with a bump. Sabrina and I spilled head first into the nearest seats. We dropped our backpacks on the floor in front of us. Sabrina began to tie her hair back in a ponytail.

She turned to me. "So? Let me guess. You were up all night thinking about Gary Steadman."

"Huh?" I gave her shoulder a hard shove. "Hel-lo? Earth calling Sabrina. I don't have a crush on Gary Steadman."

Sabrina's dark eyes flashed. "Then what did I see at Steve Boswell's party last Friday night?"

I could feel my cheeks turning hot. I knew I was blushing. I wish I could do something about that. Is there a way to learn how to keep your face from turning red?

"Sabrina, don't be a rat," I said. "Total truth? He tried to kiss me, and his braces cut my lip."

We both laughed. The bus hit a bump, and it made me hiccup.

Sabrina tugged at the brown suede waistcoat she wore over two T-shirts. She's really into clothes these days. I mainly pull on jeans and anything I can find in my T-shirt drawer.

"So, Carly Beth, if you weren't up all night thinking about The Steadman, why the dark rings under your eyes? I'm serious. You've been totally pale and droopy all day."

I sighed and stared out the stained bus window. The pavements were covered with a deep blanket

9

of brown leaves scuttling in the wind. We rolled past the library with its tall white columns. Then past Rohmer's Flower Store with a wheelbarrow of yellow and orange flowers in front.

Should I tell Sabrina the truth?

Yes, I decided. I couldn't tell anyone else about what happened last night. No one would believe it. Mom would just tell me to stop watching the Sci-Fi Channel.

But Sabrina was there that Halloween. She saw the Haunted Mask. She saw what happened to me when I wore it. Sabrina believed.

So I told her the whole story. How I woke up wide-awake at three in the morning. How I couldn't stop myself. I was pulled to the basement. Forced to open the box and take out the ugly mask.

Speaking in a hushed voice, I told her how I started to pull it down over my head. And how I finally found the strength to rip it off and shove it away.

My voice trembled as I told Sabrina how it took all my strength to stuff the screaming mask back into its box. It didn't stop screaming until I closed the box tight. And by the time I went back upstairs, it was almost time to get ready for school.

I was breathing hard when I finished telling Sabrina the story. And I could feel that my face was still bright red.

Sabrina had her hand on my arm. She shook her head. "Listen to me, Carly Beth," she whispered.

"You have to get that mask out of your house. You are *really* scaring me."

I swallowed. My mouth suddenly felt very dry. "But where can I take it?" I asked. "I don't want anyone to find it."

"Take it anywhere," Sabrina said, squeezing my arm. "Bury it in the woods. Throw it in the river."

"But . . . what if it floats?" I said. "What if someone fishes it out and puts it on? I can't let that happen to anyone else, Sabrina. It's too *horrifying*! When I wore it, it changed me. You remember. I turned angry and evil. We couldn't pull it off. The mask attached itself to my *skin*!"

"*Ssssh*." She raised a finger to her lips. "Of *course* I remember," she said. She held up both hands. Her plastic bracelets rattled. "Look. I'm shaking. I'm shaking all over. That's why you have to get that thing out of your house."

The bad memories flooded over me. "You can only defeat it with a symbol of love," I muttered.

Sabrina stared at me. "Huh?"

"Remember?" I said. "I found a symbol of love. That's the only way to remove the mask from your face and stop its evil."

Sabrina shuddered. "Can we stop talking about it? You are totally creeping me out. Change the subject. I want to hear more about Gary Steadman."

But I couldn't stop. "Only one good thing came

from that Halloween," I said. "The Haunted Mask changed me. After all that horror, I'm not the same person any more."

Sabrina rolled her eyes.

"It's *true*!" I insisted. "You remember. I was the class scaredy-cat. I was afraid of my own shadow. Really. But after defeating that evil mask, I'm different, Sabrina. I'm not scared any more."

And then something warm and dry curled around my neck.

A snake with glowing yellow eyes slid around my throat. It raised its head and opened its jaws wide.

3

The snake jerked its head back and closed its jaws.

I heard laughter behind me.

I wrapped my fingers around the snake and gently pulled it off my neck. Then I turned to the two boys in the seat behind me.

"Scared you!" Chuck Greene shouted. He and his buddy Steve Boswell hee-hawed some more and touched knuckles.

I ran my fingers up and down the snake, petting it lightly. Then I handed it back to Chuck. "I knew you brought Herbie in for science class today," I told him. "No big deal."

I twisted around in the seat so I could look at the two of them. "Your jokes are lame. Give it up, dudes. You can't scare me any more."

For some reason, they thought that was a riot. "You look like two grinning baboons," Sabrina said.

They started scratching their armpits and *eeeh eeeh eeehing* like monkeys.

Chuck and Steve aren't related, but they look like brothers. They're both tall and thin, with straight brown hair, dark brown eyes, and the same goofy grin.

They dress alike, too. They always wear baggy, faded jeans and black long-sleeve T-shirts. I don't know why. But all they want to do is scare me and make me scream. They just don't realize how different I am now.

Steve leaned over and messed up my hair. "It's almost Halloween," he said. "Are you going to hide under your bed this year till it's over?"

Chuck hee-hawed some more. Like it was a real funny joke.

Sabrina and I both rolled our eyes. "I just saw something kinda scary," I said.

"Like what?" Steve asked.

I pointed out the window. "Wasn't that your house that went by three or four streets ago?"

"Huh?" They both jumped up, grabbed their backpacks, and went running to the front of the bus. "Hey – stop! STOP!"

Sabrina and I laughed as they scrambled off the bus. We waved out the window as the bus pulled away.

"They're totally immature," Sabrina said. "Like, shouldn't they be repeating fourth grade or something?"

14

I smoothed my hair down with both hands. Then I settled back in the seat. I could still feel the chill of the snake on my neck.

Sabrina waved to someone out the window. Her plastic bracelets jangled. Then she turned and started saying something to me.

But I couldn't hear her. She sounded far away. Her voice was like an echo of an echo.

Drowned out by a high, frightening scream.

The scream of the Haunted Mask.

I struggled to hear Sabrina, but I couldn't shut out the mask's shrill wail. Couldn't shut it out. Couldn't shut it out. I covered my ears, hoping it would stop.

"What's wrong, Carly Beth?" Sabrina gripped my hands and started shaking me. "What's wrong?"

"Don't you hear it, too?" I cried.

She squinted at me. "Hear what?"

No. No. Is it inside my head now?

What am I going to do?

15

Sabrina and I climbed off the bus at the last stop. The screaming in my ears had faded, but I felt a little dizzy and weird.

I took a long, deep breath. The air smelled so fresh here at the farm on the edge of town. It smelled like cut grass and autumn leaves and flowers.

Sabrina and I started walking up the gravel path to the tall white farmhouse. The windows in the front of the house glowed red in the late afternoon sun.

The house stood in the middle of a wide green pasture. Beyond the pasture stood a big apple tree orchard.

Our shoes crunched over the gravel. We passed the red and white sign that read: TUMBLEDOWN FARMS. A cool October breeze rattled the sign.

A bunch of squawking blackbirds perched on the satellite dish behind the house. High in the sky, I saw a red hawk swoop low, then float up again. The wind made the tall pasture grass tilt one way, then the other.

"Almost Halloween," Sabrina muttered, leaning into the wind. "We have to think of some Halloween projects for the little beasts."

Our new job was helping Mrs Lange take care of eight nursery school kids in the Tumbledown Farms after-school programme.

"Don't call them beasts," I scolded. "I think they're cute."

"Cute?" Sabrina's dark eyes flashed. "Do you call stuffing crayons up your nose *cute*?"

"Only Jesse did that," I said. "And we got the crayons out with only a *little* crying, didn't we?"

"Mrs Lange says there's one bad apple in every bushel," Sabrina said.

I shook my head. "Jesse's not a bad apple. He's only five!"

"Colin is my favourite," Sabrina said. "He's like a miniature old gentleman. If you tell him to do something, he gives you a sharp salute and then he does it."

"Colin still sucks his thumb," I said.

She shrugged. "No one's perfect."

"Angela is perfect," I said. "With those red curls and green eyes, she could be a kid supermodel or something."

"Super spoiled, you mean," Sabrina replied. "The way she always has to sit in your lap?"

"She's sweet," I said. "You're just jealous."

We climbed up the wooden steps to the front porch and scraped our shoes on the welcome mat. I could hear the kids' voices inside, high and shrill. Some kind of argument. I could hear Jesse trying to outshout the others.

Tumbledown Farms is one of the oldest farms in the state. My dad told me it used to be a real working farm where they grew potatoes and tomatoes and corn and a lot of other crops. But the farm family sold it and moved away a long time ago.

Now it's a place people go to on weekends. Almost like a theme park. There's the apple orchard, a petting zoo, two restaurants, an art gallery, a big souvenir shop, hay rides and a kids' club.

I pushed open the door, and we stepped into the front room. Warm air washed over my face. I took a deep breath. The house smelled like chocolate. Mrs Lange always bakes cookies on Friday.

"Gimme it! Gimme it!" I heard Jesse shouting from the playroom.

Sabrina and I tossed our coats and backpacks down on the bench near the door and hurried to the playroom. The first thing I saw was Angela sitting at the art table, crying. An overturned cup in front of her. A big puddle of chocolate milk spreading over the table.

I turned to the window and saw Jesse and Harmony having an angry tug-of-war with a red plastic Frisbee. "Gimme it! Gimme it!" Jesse was *fierce*!

Laura Henry ran into the room, carrying a roll of paper towels. She leaned over Angela and started to mop up the spilled chocolate milk. When she saw Sabrina and me, she let out a sigh of relief.

"Thank goodness you're here!" she said. "The kids are totally wired today. I think it's a full moon or something!"

I laughed. "Laura, it's still daytime," I said.

I crossed the room to Jesse and Harmony to see if I could settle the Frisbee war. Sabrina carried some tissues over to Howard, who was screaming that he had to blow his nose.

"Where is Mrs Lange?" I asked.

"She had a problem at one of the restaurants," Laura replied. "She left me in charge." She blew a strand of hair off her forehead. "But then things got out of control."

Laura is twelve, our age. She is short and thin and has very pale white skin, silvery grey eyes, and long tangles of white-blonde hair that she's constantly pushing back or untangling or twisting around her fingers.

Today she wore a short denim skirt over black leggings. And a red and white TUMBLEDOWN FARMS sweatshirt with the sleeves rolled up to her elbows.

Laura doesn't go to our school. She goes to a private school. I think she lives close to the farm. She helps Mrs Lange with the after-school programme and a lot of other chores.

She's kind of hard to get to know. I think she's very shy.

I took the Frisbee from Jesse and Harmony and swung it behind my back. "No Frisbee in the house," I said. "Let's do something else, OK?"

Harmony spun away to join Angela at the art table. Jesse took a step back.

Suddenly, his eyes went wide and his mouth twisted in horror. He pointed up at me. "Your face!" he cried. "Carly Beth – your face! Why is it so *ugly*?"

I let out a gasp. What was he staring at?

The *mask*?

How could that *be*?

5

I staggered back. I raised my hands to my cheeks.

Jesse burst out laughing. "Gotcha!" he said. He gave me a hard shove. "Gotcha, Carly Beth." He did a crazy dance around the room, laughing like a wild man.

I felt like a total jerk. How stressed was I? I let a five-year-old frighten me.

Get a grip, Carly Beth!

Mrs Lange came trotting in. She never walks. She runs. She's a tall, heavy woman and looks older than my parents, with bright orange hair, rosy cheeks, and green eyes. She wears baggy plaid flannel shirts, long skirts down to the floor, and cowboy boots.

She is a total energy machine. I've never seen her sit down! And she talks as fast as she moves.

"What are y'all doing indoors on such a beautiful day?" she boomed. She gathered up empty drink cups. "Get outside. Smell that fresh farm air."

She picked something out of Colin's hair. She patted Angela's cheek. "I know what. Go pick apples. They're fallin' off the trees. Get the buckets behind the house. Fill 'em up, hear? Go on – get!" She practically shooed us out.

Sabrina followed me out the door. "This is a good idea," she said. "Let them blow off some steam."

Well, that's exactly what they did. The kids went tearing across the pasture, shouting and pushing one another and dancing and screaming. Sabrina and I grabbed buckets and ran after them.

"Hey – stick together!" I shouted. I followed them into the thick tangle of apple trees. "Stick together! Don't get lost!"

The air grew cooler as we moved under the shade of the trees. And the ground, thick with leaves, grew soft and squishy.

"Jesse – don't throw apples!" Sabrina shouted. "Hey – stop!"

"No throwing!" I yelled. "You could hurt somebody. Hey!"

Angela came running to me, crying and rubbing her head. "Jesse hit me!"

I hugged her and gave her head a kiss. "All better."

"Oh, yuck!" Howard was making faces, bending over something in the leaves. Other kids hurried to join him. "Oh, yuck. That's *sick*!"

I hurried over to them. Jesse was poking

something with a stick. I peered down. A rotted apple bulging with purple worms.

"Puke!" Howard groaned. "Think I'm gonna puke." He held his hand over his mouth.

I took him gently by the shoulders and moved him away. "Just don't look at it," I said. "You'll be fine."

Sabrina and I shooed everyone away from there. They took off again, shouting and spinning through the trees.

I held up two buckets in front of me. "Hey – doesn't anyone want to pick apples?"

"We came here to pick apples!" Sabrina shouted. "Hey – *anyone*?"

An apple sailed past my head. Several kids laughed.

"Stop it, Howard!" I heard Harmony shout. "That's *so* not funny!"

I couldn't see her. She stood behind the trunk of an apple tree. I could hear the crackle of leaves all around as kids ran in every direction.

"Ever get that helpless feeling?" Sabrina asked me.

I laughed. "You were right. They *are* beasts. At least today."

We followed the kids through the trees to the far side of the orchard. Some of them were jumping over a low wooden fence that had fallen over. A field of tall grass and weeds stretched beyond the fence.

And in a corner of the field. . .

I squinted into the late afternoon sun, a red ball just above the trees.

"What *is* that?" I asked Sabrina, who stepped up beside me. "It looks like a long house or shed. But what would a house be doing way back here?"

"It's a stable," Sabrina said. She shielded her eyes from the sun with one hand. "It's been abandoned for years. It's falling down."

Yes. The windows were all broken. One wall had fallen in. Part of the shingled roof had collapsed.

I turned and saw Howard and Jesse darting across the field, pulling Harmony with them. They were heading for the empty stable.

"Come back!" Sabrina shouted. "Hey – you guys! Come back!"

They giggled and kept running. Several other kids began to follow them.

I cupped my hands around my mouth to shout to them. But I stopped when I heard the sound.

I listened hard. Was that a horse whinny?

From the abandoned stable?

Impossible, I told myself. But there – I heard it again.

I poked Sabrina in the side. "Did you hear that?"

She frowned at me. "Hear what?"

"I thought I heard something. A horse maybe. Let's go check out the old stable," I said. I started pushing through the tall grass.

"No. Wait." Sabrina grabbed my arm and held me back. "Carly Beth, I know you love horses. But the stable looks dangerous. It's falling down. We should stop the kids. We have to get them back to Mrs Lange."

"Come on. We'll just take a quick peek," I said.

I grabbed Sabrina's hand and started to drag her through the field. We didn't get far.

After five or six steps, we both heard a frightened voice yell from behind us:

"NOOOOOOOO! DON'T GO THERE!"

I spun around. Laura stood behind us at the edge of the apple orchard. Her blonde hair blew wildly around her face. She waved frantically, shouting for us to come back.

So Sabrina and I rounded up the kids. They were pretty easy to herd back. The long walk and all the running and screaming had them tired out.

Their parents and babysitters were waiting in the front room to take them home. Sabrina, Laura and I stuffed them into their coats and hats, and they were gone.

Silence.

The only sounds now were the rattle of the old windows against the wind and the steady ticking of the grandfather clock in the front hallway.

The three of us cleaned up the playroom. Then we headed to the kitchen. It was an enormous old farmhouse kitchen with a wide window along the back of the house, looking out on the pasture.

Laura had a pot of hot chocolate on the stove. She poured it into tall white mugs. We sat down to sip it and relax at the kitchen table with its red-and-white-chequered tablecloth.

"So, what's the deal with the abandoned stable?" I asked. "Why did you yell like that?"

Laura slowly twirled her mug between her pale hands. "Don't you know about that old stable?" she asked us in a hushed voice.

A hard gust of wind rattled the kitchen window.

Sabrina and I shook our heads. "We never walked there before," I said.

Laura nodded. She took a sip of hot chocolate. "It's a scary story," she said. "Mrs Lange told me the whole thing. It's actually very sad."

I leaned forward. "A scary story? What do you mean?"

Laura curled a strand of hair between her fingers. She kept her eyes on the window. "It was a riding stable many years ago," she started. "Very popular. With beautiful horses. Well cared for and well groomed."

She took another sip from her mug and held it between her hands. "One night, people in the farmhouse heard screams. High-pitched shrieks and screams. Not human screams. They knew they couldn't be human screams."

27

I suddenly had a cold feeling in the pit of my stomach. "What do you mean? Who was screaming?" I asked.

"The screams were shrill and frightened," Laura continued. "They came from the stable. The horses were screaming." She twisted and untwisted her hair. "I've never heard a horse scream. Have you?"

I swallowed. "It . . . it must have been *terrifying*. But—"

"Everyone went running to the stable. They pulled open the doors and found the horses dead," Laura said. "All of them. Lying against the wall in a heap. All dead."

"Huh?" I gasped. "Why? What killed them?"

"Panic," Laura replied. "They all died from fear."

Sabrina had her hands up to her cheeks. Her dark eyes were wide with horror. "But – why?" she asked.

Wind rattled the window again. I shivered.

I love horses. I wanted to work after school in the stable near my house. But they didn't have a job for me. So I ended up at Tumbledown Farms.

"The stable boy was blamed," Laura said. "He sneaked into the stable one night. They think he wanted to scare the horse groomer. Or maybe someone else in the stable."

"But he scared the horses instead?" I asked.

Laura nodded. "You could hear them screeching

and wailing for miles. They went insane. They were locked inside the stable. But they stampeded. They crushed each other against the door, against the stable walls. The stable boy fell under their hooves and was kicked to death."

"Oh, wow," I muttered.

I glanced across the table at Sabrina. She hadn't taken a sip of her hot chocolate. She had her eyes down.

"That's the story, according to Mrs Lange," Laura said. "I warned you it was sad. Can you *imagine* opening the stable door and finding the horses in a heap – dead?"

I swallowed hard. "But how exactly did he scare the horses?" I asked.

Laura let out a long breath. Her face was even paler than usual. "You'll never believe it," she said. "The farmers claimed it was all caused by a mask, a hideous Halloween mask."

Laura shook her head. "But when they cleaned up the stable, the ugly mask was nowhere to be found. It totally disappeared."

I heard a *thud*. I was so upset by Laura's story, I didn't even realize I'd knocked over my hot chocolate mug. The hot liquid ran down my jeans.

"Carly Beth, are you OK?"

I heard Sabrina, but I was too deep in thought to answer.

"Carly Beth? Are you OK? Carly Beth?"

7

Could she be talking about the same mask?

My heart pounded in my chest. I pictured the mask – so hideous with its wrinkled, warty green flesh, its crooked rows of jagged fangs.

I glanced up. Sabrina was mopping up the spilled hot chocolate. She put a hand on my shoulder. "Earth calling Carly Beth," she whispered.

I blinked. And focused on Laura. "Did Mrs Lange tell you anything else about the stable boy's mask?" I asked her.

She shook her head. "No. Just that there's a legend about it. About how it always appears at Halloween time."

That sent a chill down the back of my neck.

Laura narrowed her silvery grey eyes at me. "Why are you so interested, Carly Beth?"

"It . . . it's just so sad," I stammered.

"Know what's weird?" Sabrina said. "Carly Beth said she heard a horse whinny. In that old stable."

Laura squinted at me. "No way. That's part of the story. That the ghosts of the horses remain in the stable."

"She heard a horse," Sabrina insisted. "Definitely a horse whinny. Right, Carly Beth?"

Before I could answer, Mrs Lange came bursting in. Her arms were loaded down with firewood logs. She dumped them in front of the old potbellied stove at the back of the kitchen.

"Are y'all talking about our famous haunted stable?" she asked. She wiped her hands off on her long skirt. Then she grabbed a mug and emptied the hot chocolate pot into it.

"It's fun to tell ghost stories at Halloween," she said. "I don't believe in ghosts. But you know what everyone says, don't you? That the old stable is haunted – by those poor horses – and by the stable boy?"

We stared at her. "You mean, the stable boy's ghost is still there?" I asked.

Mrs Lange nodded. "They say he won't leave until he gets his Halloween mask back."

I couldn't help myself. I let out a sharp cry.

Across the table, Laura stared at me. "What's wrong, Carly Beth?" she asked.

Mrs Lange laughed. "Maybe Carly Beth just doesn't like ghost stories," she said.

"Right," I said. My face suddenly felt hot. "Scary stories always give me nightmares."

I jumped up. "Come on, Sabrina. The bus will be here any minute."

Sabrina and I hurried to put on our coats. As we walked down the gravel path to the road, I knew we were both asking ourselves the same questions:

Did the stable boy have the same mask all those years ago? The mask that's in my basement? And was the boy's ghost in the abandoned stable, waiting to get it back?

At dinner, I couldn't stop thinking about Laura's story. About the poor horses screaming their heads off. Stampeding into the wall and dying in a horrible panic.

About the mask . . . the ugly, terrifying mask.

"Carly Beth, are you awake?" Dad asked. "Didn't you hear me asking about your job?"

"Uh . . . no. Sorry," I muttered.

"Maybe she's a zombie," my little brother, Noah, said. "Let's see. . ." He pinched my arm really hard.

"Hey!" I jerked my arm away. "Give me a break, Noah!"

Noah giggled and tried to pinch me again.

"Brat! You're worse than the five-year-olds!" I said.

"You're worse than the *four*-year-olds!" he said.

"Ooh. Clever!"

"Those kids must have run you ragged today," Mom said. She reached over and smoothed back my hair.

"Yeah. They were pretty wild," I muttered.

"You're worse than the *two*-year-olds!" Noah said, and giggled some more.

"Can I be excused?" I asked.

I hurried up to my room. I had a lot of homework. But I couldn't concentrate on it. I kept worrying about the Haunted Mask.

I thought about last night. How it pulled me down to the basement against my will. How it forced me to take it out of its hiding place. How it almost made me pull it down over my head.

How it screamed . . . screamed . . . screamed.

I was so totally freaked last night. Such a close call.

Did I leave the metal box open? Did I lock it away?

I couldn't remember.

I paced back and forth in my room. Thinking hard. Thinking about the boy in the stable. The horses. The mask in the basement.

I realized I had no choice. I had to make sure the mask was safely tucked in its hiding place. I had to be sure the box was locked tight.

I crept out of my room and made my way down to the basement stairs. I could hear Mom and Dad in the den. They were shouting and cheering as guns fired and bombs exploded.

My parents recently discovered video games. Almost every night after dinner, they were in front of the widescreen TV, playing *WarMaster II* in high def.

Totally weird.

I gripped the handle to the basement door and took a deep breath. I didn't want to go down there. The scream of the mask still echoed in my ears.

But I had to make sure I had locked it away.

I pulled open the door, clicked on the basement light, and started down the steep wooden stairs. Again, they creaked under my feet.

I made it halfway down. I could hear the loud hum of the furnace. And then, over that hum, I heard. . .

. . . a *whisper*?

I sucked in a deep breath. And listened.

Yes. A whispered voice, harsh and raspy:

"Carly Beth . . . Carly Beth . . . I'm here, Carly Beth!"

A scream burst from my throat. My legs started to buckle. I grabbed the banister to keep from falling.

The furnace hum turned into a roar in my ears. I struggled to hear the whispered voice.

Silence now.

Silence.

And then a high-pitched giggle.

I gasped. "Noah!"

He stepped into the light at the bottom of the stairs and did a crazy dance.

"Noah! That's not funny!" I choked angrily. I ran down the rest of the stairs and wrapped my hands around his scrawny neck. "I could strangle you, you creep!"

He giggled some more and ducked out of my grasp.

"What are you doing down here?" I cried.

He grinned at me. "You're always telling people

35

how brave you are, Carly Beth. But I heard you scream."

"Did not!" I shouted.

"Did too!"

"I just screamed to give you a thrill," I said.

"Yeah. Right." He rolled his eyes. Then he pushed me out of the way and darted up the stairs. "Bye, chicken!" He slammed the basement door behind him.

I stood there, gazing around the basement, waiting for my heart to stop racing.

Was Noah right? Am I brave now? Or am I just pretending?

No. Stop thinking about it, I told myself.

I *wanted* to be brave. I didn't want to be the scaredy-cat Carly Beth from last year.

I pushed my hair out of my eyes, took another deep breath, and started across the basement to the storage room.

I stopped when I passed my horse posters on the playroom wall. The horses were so beautiful. Once again, I pictured the horrifying stampede of screaming horses in that old stable.

Would I ever be able to get that story out of my mind?

I stepped slowly into the storage room and pulled the string to turn on the ceiling bulb. Blinking in the yellow light, I hurried to the pile of cartons in the corner.

Oh, no.

The black metal box. It sat on the basement floor in front of the cartons. Last night, I locked the mask back inside. But I was so freaked, I didn't hide the box away.

Now I bent down and lifted it off the floor with both hands.

"Hey!" I let out a sharp cry. The mask! It was bumping against the sides of the box. Trying to escape.

And this time, the whispered words didn't come from Noah. They came from *inside* the box.

"Almost Halloween. . . Almost Halloween. . ."

A few days later, on Saturday afternoon, I was home babysitting Noah. So far, he wasn't any trouble. He was in his room, and I could hear him laughing. He was watching the shows he thinks are so hilarious on the Disney Channel.

I was sitting in my room, staring at a bottle of hair colour I'd bought at the chemist. My plan was to put some blonde highlights in my hair. A bold move.

Maybe too bold. I decided to wait and talk to Sabrina about it.

The phone rang, and it was Sabrina. "Did you hear about Sara David?"

Sara is a girl in our class who changes her hair colour all the time. And she told us she's been wearing lipstick since she was five.

"What about Sara?" I asked.

"She went to the mall to buy a birthday present for her mother, and she got her nose pierced," Sabrina said.

"That's a weird birthday present!" I said. We both laughed.

"She has a tiny little diamond in her nose," Sabrina said.

"Does her mother know? Did Sara ask her first?" I asked.

"No," Sabrina replied. "She's not going to say anything. Sara says no one ever pays any attention to her. She's going to wait and see if anyone in her family notices."

"Cool," I said.

I heard Noah laughing his head off in the next room.

"I had an idea," Sabrina said.

"You're going to get your nose pierced?" I asked.

"No. About school. You know that report we have to write? About local legends? I think I'm going to write mine about that abandoned stable."

I pictured the old stable. The walls falling in. Tall grass growing over the doors.

"Such a creepy story. It will make a good report," Sabrina said. "I'm going to interview Mrs Lange next week. And I want to go take pictures inside the stable."

"Inside?" I said.

"Yes. You know. All the empty stalls," Sabrina said. "Come with me. OK? Want to go now?"

"I can't," I said. "I'm babysitting the Noah Animal."

I started to say I didn't want to go back to that stable anyway. But I quickly changed my mind. This was the perfect time to *prove* that I was over my fears.

"How about tonight after dinner?" Sabrina asked.

"Sure," I said. "Meet you at the bus stop."

I took a deep breath. It was just an abandoned stable.

What could happen?

10

The sun was dropping behind the trees as Sabrina and I rode the bus to the edge of town. I watched the shadows creep over the passing houses and lawns.

We climbed off the bus at Tumbledown Farms. I saw only one light on in an upstairs window of the farmhouse. We turned away from the gravel path and made our way around the apple orchard.

Insects buzzed in the field behind the house. I led the way to the stable, pushing the tall grass aside to make a path for us. The hard earth crunched under our shoes.

I heard animals scampering through the dry grass and weeds. The sky grew darker. Clouds covered the moon. I shivered as a gust of cold wind blew inside my jacket.

"I brought a flashlight," Sabrina said. I heard a click, and a circle of white light swept over the grass. "Look. There's the stable." She raised the light higher.

I could see the long, low building, black against the pink-grey sky.

"Ow!" I cried out as a sharp pain stung my forehead. A mosquito? In October? I slapped at it. Too late.

"Come on. It's getting really dark," Sabrina said. She started to run. The beam of light bounced on the ground in front of her.

"Wait up!" I called. My eyes were on the stable. The boards on one wall were cracked and rotting away. Another wall had fallen in.

Weeds grew out of the windows. The window shutters were all broken and tilting to the ground.

We hurried along the side of the stable towards the front. I stopped when my shoes sank into something soft. "Sabrina – look!" I called. But she was at the doors and didn't hear me.

I stared down at my shoes. I was standing in a small square of soft, chunky earth. It looked as if it had been freshly dug up.

A disturbing thought flashed into my mind: *it's a small grave.*

But that was crazy. Who would dig a grave back here?

I kicked the earth off my shoes and joined Sabrina at the double doors. One door was wide open. Solid blackness inside. And the sour smell of straw and earth and decay.

I could feel my heart start to pound a little harder. Birds cried in the trees behind us, as if warning us to stay away. I heard the low *hoot hoot* of a barn owl.

I grabbed Sabrina's arm.

"What's wrong?" she asked.

"I . . . brought something," I said. I held up the plastic bag I'd been carrying. I pulled out a bunch of carrots.

Sabrina raised the flashlight. "Carrots? Carly Beth – why?"

I shrugged. "I don't know why," I said. "For the ghost horses, I guess."

She rolled her eyes. "Are you getting weird or what? You don't really believe in ghost horses – do you?"

I didn't answer. I took Sabrina's hand and pulled her through the open door, into the dark stable.

The sour smell grew stronger. The air felt heavy – cold and damp. Like stepping into a refrigerator.

The wind banged a shutter against the side of the stable. Our shoes slid on dry straw as we walked towards the horse stalls. I tripped over a metal bucket and sent it rolling across the earth floor.

"Careful," Sabrina whispered. She handed me the flashlight. "Hold this while I take pictures." She raised her camera and clicked it on.

I set the bunch of carrots down in front of the first stall. Then I swept the flashlight beam around the stable.

The light rolled over two rows of stalls with low wooden walls. They stretched all the way to the back of the stable.

A shredded blanket lay over one of the stall walls. It looked as if animals had chewed it to tatters.

A high mound of straw was piled inside the first stall. I lowered the light to it, and a fat brown mouse leaped out and scurried under the wall.

Startled, I jumped back. The light bounced up to the stable roof. Were those bats clinging upside down to the low rafters?

Sabrina was busy flashing photo after photo. I pointed to the ceiling, and she flashed some pictures of the bats.

"Over here," she whispered. We made our way down the row of stalls. The air grew warmer and damper as we stepped deeper into the stable.

"Carly Beth, move the light," Sabrina said. "Check that out."

She pointed to a tall wooden stool lying on its side on the stable floor. She picked it up, set it down, and dusted it off with one hand.

"Do you think the stable boy sat on this stool?" she asked. "Wouldn't that be totally weird?"

She didn't give me a chance to answer. She climbed on to the stool and shoved the camera into my hands. "Take my picture sitting on this. It will be great for the front of my report."

I raised the camera to my eye and clicked the shutter. The flash caught Sabrina sitting on the stool with both hands raised above her head in triumph.

I flashed another one. The burst of light lingered in my eyes. I tried to blink it away.

The tall stool appeared to glow in the lingering circle of light. Did the poor stable boy sit on that stool so long ago? Did it get knocked over in the stampede of panicked horses?

I tried to force those thoughts from my mind.

And then I heard a *thud*. A bumping sound from one of the back stalls.

"Sabrina – did you hear that?" My voice came out in a hushed whisper.

She froze beside me. "Yes. I . . . I heard it," she whispered.

We both stood still, listening hard.

A shiver ran down my neck. "I have this weird feeling," I murmured. "Like we're being watched."

"It had to be a mouse or a raccoon or something," Sabrina said.

Another bump. And then I heard the rustle of straw.

Then I heard something that sent a cold shudder down my spine.

11

The low whinny of a horse.

The flashlight fell out of my hand and clunked on the stable floor. I grabbed Sabrina's arm. "You heard it, too?"

Before she could answer – another horse whinny, louder this time. So close. So very close. From a stall near the back of the stable.

"Yes. I hear it, too," Sabrina whispered. She huddled close to me.

We heard another bump. Like a horse bumping up against a stall wall. And then the rustle and scrape of hooves in straw.

"The ghost story!" I whispered. "It's *true*!" I was shaking. My throat closed up. I struggled to breathe.

"It's true, Sabrina. It's *all* true!" I squeezed her arm.

To my surprise, Sabrina burst out laughing. She stepped away from me.

46

"Sabrina?"

"I'm sorry, Carly Beth," she said, shaking her head. "I can't keep up the joke any more. It's too mean."

I was still shaking. I hugged myself, wrapping my arms around me. "Joke?"

Sabrina cupped her hands around her mouth and shouted. "OK, Chuck and Steve! You can come out now!"

OK. OK. I started to get it. I started to figure out what was going on here.

Sabrina grabbed my shoulder. "You don't have to worry about ghost horses. It's just another joke, Carly Beth," she said. "It was Chuck's idea. I'm sorry. They made me bring you here. I thought it would be funny."

My breathing slowly returned to normal. I wasn't afraid any more. I was *angry*. What was their *problem*?

"OK, dudes!" Sabrina shouted. "Where are you? Joke's over. You can come out now!"

She swung the flashlight around, beaming it from stall to stall.

Silence. Except for the wind whistling through the cracks in the walls.

"Chuck? Steve?" I called. "Very funny. Ha-ha. See? I'm laughing! You guys are a riot!"

Silence. No sign of them.

"We know you're in here," Sabrina said.

47

I tugged Sabrina towards the back. "Come on. Those two jerks want to play hide-and-seek. Let's find them."

We started at the rear stalls. Sabrina aimed the light and moved it around in each stall. A blackened saddle was half buried under a pile of straw in the first stall. The second stall had a dead field mouse, it's body nearly eaten away by insects, its tiny skull poking out.

"Come on. Come out, guys!" Sabrina shouted. "Joke's over!"

We moved quickly down the row of stalls till we were back where we started at the front of the stable. Sabrina frowned at me. "Where are they hiding? I know they're here."

She lowered the flashlight.

I glanced down – and gasped. "Sabrina – look! The carrots are gone!"

12

I hugged myself to stop from shaking. "Sabrina, something very weird is going on here," I whispered.

"No, it isn't," she replied. Now she sounded angry. "Chuck and Steve took the carrots. I know they did. I don't believe those two creeps." She glanced around. "Where are they?"

"Maybe they sneaked past us," I said. "They grabbed the carrots and ran out of the stable while we were at the back."

"Maybe," Sabrina said. She pulled her mobile phone from her jeans pocket. "Let's see. I'll call Chuck."

I held the flashlight for her. She punched Chuck's number on her phone. A few seconds later, she said. "Hey. Chuck? It's Sabrina. Where are you?"

A pause. Then: "You're home? What do you *mean* you're home? Steve is there, too? But what about the joke you wanted to play? Remember? Carly Beth? The old stable?"

Standing next to Sabrina, I could hear Chuck's loud groan pour out of the phone.

Sabrina turned to me. "Do you believe it?" she said. "They're both at Chuck's house. It was *their* joke – and they forgot all about it!" She clicked her phone shut.

I staggered back. My brain was spinning. If the boys weren't here, who made the horse sounds? Sabrina and I both heard them. The low whinnying. The thud of hooves on straw.

Sabrina chewed her bottom lip. Her dark eyes were wide. "I . . . think maybe I'm afraid now," she murmured. "Let's get out of here!"

We both took off running. Through the open stable door. Across the field, the tall weeds and grass slapping at us as we ran.

The harsh October wind forced us to lower our heads. Our shoes slipped and slid over patches of wet mud and grassy ground.

Again I heard the low *hoot hoot* of an owl somewhere close by.

And louder than the owl . . . another horse whinny. This time, shrill and pleading, as if calling after us.

EEE-EEEE-EEEEEE!

"Noooooo!" Sabrina and I both screamed as we tore through the field. Running full speed, our arms flying out at our sides, we screamed all the way to the bus stop at the road.

Our wet shoes thudded on the pavement. We fell on each other, leaned on each other, breathing hard. Panting. The shrill horse cry still fresh in our ears.

"Come on, bus," I said, my eyes on the dark road. "Come on, bus – hurry!"

"Where *is* that bus?" Sabrina groaned.

The trees along the road creaked and shook in the wind. The clouds rolled away from the moon. Pale silver light floated down.

I turned back. I could see the dark stable in the moonlight.

I let out a cry when I saw the boy. A boy crouched on the flat stable roof. He was staring at us. Not moving. Just staring at us.

I couldn't move. I stood there staring back at him.

How did he get up there? Did he make those noises?

Who *is* he?

13

"Jesse, did you take some of Colin's Legos?" I held Jesse by the shoulders and gazed into his eyes.

He looked away. "Maybe. But I needed them to finish my robot," he said.

"You wrecked *my* robot!" Colin cried. "And my robot was better than yours!"

"Your robot looked like a *rabbit*!" Jesse shouted.

"Did not! Your robot looked like a *skunk*!"

Sabrina took Colin by the hand and led him to the table where the plastic blocks were scattered. She sat down beside him, and they started to build a new robot together.

"Jesse, are you going to apologize to Colin?" I asked softly.

He made a face at me. Then he yelled to Colin: "I'm sorry your robot looked like a dumb bunny rabbit!"

Nice apology.

After the kids had left, Mrs Lange helped

Sabrina, Laura and me clean up. "I have to ask you something," she said, shoving handfuls of Legos back into the box. "Can you girls work on Halloween?"

We stopped and stared at her. "You mean Halloween night? What's up?" I asked.

"The parents asked if we could have a party here for the kids," she replied. "You know. Give them a nice, safe Halloween. Costumes, food, games. The whole deal. They're willing to pay extra. And it will be early. You'll still have plenty of time to go out afterwards."

"I can do it," Laura said, brushing back her hair with both hands. "No problem."

"Me, too," Sabrina said. "Get paid for Halloween? That's awesome!"

"Count me in," I said. After the horror of last year, a safe Halloween night with little kids sounded excellent to me.

"I love Halloween parties," Laura said. "Maybe we can have a jack-o'-lantern contest. And . . . I know! The kids can make their own masks. They'd like that – right?"

"I like your enthusiasm," Mrs Lange said. She grabbed a broom and started to sweep the floor. "Carly Beth, maybe you know some good ghost stories you can tell the kids."

"Whoa." I shook my head. "I keep thinking about the ghost of the stable boy. Too creepy. Maybe we could skip the ghost stories this year!"

We said good night to Mrs Lange. Sabrina had to get home early because some cousins were coming for dinner. Laura headed home, too.

I couldn't help myself. I walked out of the back door and started towards the apple orchard. I knew where I was going. To the abandoned stable. I couldn't stop myself. I had to see it again.

The sun had already dropped behind the trees. It was a clear, cool evening.

I crossed the field through the tall grass swaying in the soft breeze. I walked along the side of the stable until I came to the patch of freshly dug earth.

I gazed at it. What a puzzle. Someone was digging on this spot recently. But who? And why?

No way to answer those questions. I stepped around the square of earth and hurried into the stable.

The sharp smell of hay and mud greeted me. Grey light slanted in through the small stable windows and through a large hole in the roof.

I glanced around quickly. The stable was empty. I saw the tattered blanket over the stall wall. And low piles of straw along one wall with thousands of little insects crawling over them.

I turned to leave. But I froze when I heard a scraping sound.

Hooves in the straw? No. It sounded more like human footsteps.

I spun around. And shouted: "Is anyone here?"

Silence.

And then another scraping sound.

My eyes searched each stall. I knew I wasn't alone. But I couldn't see anyone.

"Oh!" I uttered a cry as a boy appeared beside me.

He had dark brown hair cut very short. And deep black eyes. They appeared even darker because of his pale skin.

He wore a brown and black flannel shirt and torn jeans.

"Who are you?" I cried, stepping away from him. "What are you doing here?"

A strange lopsided smile spread over his face. "I live here," he said.

14

"I . . . I don't understand," I stammered. I couldn't stop staring into those deep, sad eyes. "No one lives here. This stable. . ."

The boy shook his head. The lopsided smile lingered on his face. "I mean, my family lives nearby," he said. He spoke slowly, with a slight drawl. "I come here a lot," he said, "because it's so peaceful."

I had a sudden urge to reach out and grab him. Grab his arm. See if it was solid. See if he was real.

"What are *you* doing here?" he asked.

"I . . . I work at the farm. After school, I mean. With kids." I was stammering like an idiot. He could see I was kind of freaked. "My name is Carly Beth."

"I'm Clark," he said. "I think I scared you, popping out like that. Sorry."

"It's OK," I said.

"Do you know the story of this stable?" he asked. "It's a pretty scary place." He laughed. "Maybe that's why I like to come here." His eyes burned into mine. "Think it's twisted to like scary things?"

His question sent a chill down my back. Maybe it was the way he asked it, staring at me like he could read my mind or something.

"I . . . heard the story," I replied. "It's horrible. Those poor horses. . ."

He frowned at me. "Excuse me? You care more about the horses? What about the stable boy?"

"It . . . it's all horrible," I choked out. "You know, my friend Sabrina and I were here last Saturday. And we . . . we heard horses. Whinnying here in this stable."

Clark laughed. He had a funny laugh. Kind of dry. It sounded like he was choking.

"You must have a good imagination," he said. "I come here all the time. And I never hear horses. Field mice, maybe. But never horses."

"It wasn't field mice," I said. "That I know for sure."

He kicked a pile of straw. Hundreds of insects went swarming across the stable floor. "Such a sad place," he said softly. "It's weird to think about it."

I wondered if Clark knew anything about the mask. I was dying to know if the stable boy's mask was the same evil mask I had in my basement.

"They say it was a scary mask that started the stampede," I said.

Clark's eyes flashed. His expression turned serious.

"Do you know what the mask looked like?" I asked.

He shrugged. "Beats me."

He's lying, I decided.

And then the words just blurted out of my mouth. I don't know why. But I started to tell him the story of what happened to me last Halloween.

"I . . . I asked you about the mask because I had a bad time last Halloween with an evil mask," I started.

Again his eyes locked on mine. I definitely had his attention.

"Last year," I continued, "when I put the mask on, it stuck to my skin. I couldn't pull it off. And it started to change me. I suddenly had evil thoughts. Horrible, evil thoughts. The mask – it was taking over my brain and—"

Clark laughed. He brushed a hand back through his short brown hair. "An evil mask?" he said. "You're joking – right?"

I shook my head. "No, Clark, I'm totally serious. I—"

He laughed again. "Give me a break," he said. "A mask that turns you evil?"

I crossed my arms in front of me. "You said you know the story of the stable boy," I said. "Then you know that he wore an evil mask that frightened the horses. And now they say the boy haunts this stable. He—"

Clark gaped at me. "Carly Beth – you believe in *ghosts*?" he cried. "No way. You believe in ghosts and evil masks?" He laughed. "Is your friend Sabrina as weird as you are?"

I stared back at him. I could tell he was lying. He was only pretending not to believe me. It was obvious. He was putting on a big show. Like he didn't believe in ghosts or haunted masks.

I felt another chill. He was kind of cute. But there was something strange about him. Something he was hiding.

Why was he hanging out here in this smelly, bug-infested stable? And why was he dressed like a stable boy in that old flannel shirt?

"I . . . have to go," I said. "It's late. I don't want to miss the next bus."

He grinned. "Hope the bus isn't *haunted*!" His dark eyes flashed.

I rolled my eyes. "Very funny," I said. "Well . . . nice meeting you, Clark. See you around . . . I guess."

"See you." He gave me a quick two-fingered salute.

I spun away and jogged out of the stable. The

air felt so cool and fresh as soon as I got out of the smelly stable. I trotted across the field to the road.

And then, over the thuds of my trainers on the hard ground, I heard shrill sounds. Horses whinnying behind me.

Horse cries, so sad. Calling me. Calling me back to that frightening stable.

15

I ran to the road. The horse cries rang in my ears. Breathing hard, I grabbed the bus stop pole and held it tightly, struggling to catch my breath.

A car rolled by with loud country music blaring out the window. The sun had dropped low behind the trees. Strange shadows rolled across the field, like living creatures.

The road was dark. No sign of the bus. It ran every half hour or so. But I wanted it to be there *now*.

I wanted to get away. Away from that stable with the strange boy inside. The boy with the deep, dark eyes, who laughed at me when I said I heard horses. Who laughed when I said the stable was haunted.

What was the truth about Clark?

I shuddered as the sky grew even darker. I didn't want to think about Clark or ghosts or masks. I wanted to get AWAY from here!

"The bus is *never* coming," I muttered.

I should have gone home with Sabrina, I told myself. *I never should have wandered over to that stable.*

I grabbed my mobile phone. I decided to see if Mom or Dad could come pick me up. I started to punch in our number – and stopped.

My phone was dead. No power.

With a loud sigh, I pushed the phone back into my jeans pocket.

A bird cackled loudly in a tree across the road. "Are you laughing at me?" I called to it.

I decided to start walking. I'd walk along the road towards home. When the bus came, I'd wave at it to stop.

Or I could walk the whole way. It was only a kilometre or two.

It will feel good to walk, I told myself. *It will give me a chance to think. A chance to figure things out in my mind.*

I had a lot to think about. As I trudged along the gravel on the side of the road, my mind was spinning.

Did I really hear ghost horses?

Was it my Haunted Mask that caused the stampede that killed them all?

I knew Sabrina was right. I had to get that mask out of my basement. But where could I take it? Where could I hide it where no one would ever find it?

The walk took longer than I'd thought. I checked

62

my watch. Nearly seven o'clock. Dinner was at six thirty. Mom and Dad would be frantic by now.

They were probably calling my dead mobile and calling Mrs Lange. When they found out I walked home, they would go ballistic!

The air grew cooler. I zipped my jacket to the top. My backpack suddenly felt as if it weighed a thousand pounds.

The farm fields gave way to rows of small houses. I knew I was almost there. I wiped sweat off my forehead with the back of my hand and kept walking.

"Look out!" a voice cried.

Two boys on bikes roared past me, one on each side. They laughed and slapped a high five, happy that they scared me.

Most of the houses were brightly lit. Inside, I could see people sitting at dinner tables. In one front window, a huge white cat stared at me as I walked past.

If only I could call Mom and Dad and let them know I was OK. I pulled my phone out again and shook it. No. No power.

I reached Melrose Street and turned the corner on to Deckland. I was ten or fifteen minutes from home.

A large grey dog jumped up in its driveway and began barking at me ferociously. My heart skipped a beat. Then I saw the dog was on a chain.

I turned another corner and found myself on a street of small stores. I saw a laundry and a shoe repair store, both closed for the night. I passed the post office and a small pizza takeout restaurant.

I started to cross the street – then stopped in the middle.

I stared at the store on the next corner. Stared into the bright orange light in its window.

Faces stared back at me. Ugly, twisted faces. Masks.

Three rows of Halloween masks gazed out of the store window. I saw a gorilla mask, several monster masks with bulging eyes and blood-dripping fangs, a furry werewolf mask, a creature with its skull poking out the top of its head. . .

Frozen in the middle of the street, I stared from mask to mask. Then my eyes went to the glass door in the front.

A chill shook my body.

I recognized the store. I *knew* it so well. The store appeared in so many of my nightmares.

The mask store.

The store where I'd bought the Haunted Mask!

16

How could it be here? How could it be back?

The store had vanished. Disappeared without a trace, leaving an empty plot behind.

So how could I be staring at it now?

A loud blast from a car horn shocked me out of my daze. I shielded my eyes from the headlights and hurried across the street.

I stepped into the orange glow of the store window. The ugly masks gazed out at me.

I ran to the front door and grabbed the handle. The store was real. It wasn't a dream.

I pressed my face to the glass and peered inside. I could see the narrow aisle with long shelves of masks on both sides. Just as I remembered it.

And behind the counter – the same strange man. The man who'd sold me the Haunted Mask.

He stood there, reading a book. He raised his face to the light, and I could see him clearly.

He had the same slicked-down black hair parted in the middle. The same pencil-thin black moustache. He wore a flowing black cape over a black suit.

I stood for a long while with my hand on the door handle, watching him. Remembering his little black eyes. The way he seemed to see into my thoughts. . .

I took a deep breath and gave the door a hard tug. It swung open so fast, I nearly banged into it. Stumbling, I stepped into the store.

He didn't look up. He waited for me to step up to the counter. Then he raised his head slowly and squinted at me with those strange little eyes.

"Do you remember me?" I asked in a high, shrill voice.

He nodded. "Of course I remember you, Carly Beth."

That made my pulse race. I didn't like him saying my name.

I gripped the counter with both hands to stop myself from shaking. "You must take back the mask! You MUST!" I shouted.

An unpleasant smile spread under his thin moustache. "Take it back? How?" he asked. He closed his book and set it down on the counter.

It was an old, tattered book. I saw the title on the cover: *New Faces*.

"It's in my basement," I said. "I'll bring it to you. Tonight."

The smile faded. "You can't return it," he said. Behind him, a shelf of human skulls grinned at me.

"Why NOT?" I screamed.

He brushed back his cape. "You think you defeated it the first time," he said softly. "But I know the truth."

My mouth dropped open. "Huh? The truth?"

He drew closer, so close I could smell his sour breath. "The mask doesn't accept defeat," he whispered.

"That's c-crazy!" I stammered.

"It will be back, Carly Beth," he said. "It will come after you this Halloween. And there's nothing that I can do about it."

"That's CRAZY!" I cried. "I have it locked up. I—"

He brought his face up to mine. "No one has *ever* defeated the mask. No one whose skin became the mask's skin, whose eyes became the mask's eyes, has lived to tell about it. The mask destroyed them. All of them. All of them, except *you*. You are alive . . . *for now!*"

He took a step back and let out a long sigh. "Do you think you are the only victim of the mask? Someone else is out there, Carly Beth. Someone else owned the mask and will do anything to get it back. *Anything.* Someone you know."

"Huh?" My mouth dropped open. "You . . . you're

confusing me," I said. "Just tell me what I can do. Please!"

"I cannot tell you because I do not know. But I do know this," he said. "The mask will not quit until it controls you. Until it fills you once again with its evil."

"No! Please—" I begged. "Please!"

He shrugged. His cape rustled behind him. "I tried to warn you, Carly Beth. I tried to stop you. But you wouldn't listen. You bought the mask and ran off with it. And now you must pay a most painful price."

"No! Listen to me!" I cried. "I'll bring it back right now. You can lock it away in your store."

He shook his head. "Sorry."

He slid quickly from behind the counter. He took my arm. His fingers pinched my skin. He led me out the door.

"No. Please! Wait! Help me!" I cried.

I was standing outside. I heard a lock click. The store went dark.

I let out a sharp cry. "No! You've got to help me!" I screamed.

I grabbed the door. It wouldn't budge. I started to pound it with both fists.

"I don't want the mask! Take it back!" I screamed. "Take it back! Take it back! Take it back!"

17

I ran the rest of the way home. The stores . . . the houses . . . street after street of trees and gardens . . . just a blur of grey and black.

I was panting hard when I finally pulled myself up my driveway. I crept in through the back door. The house felt so warm. I could smell roast chicken.

Mom and Dad were in the den. I tossed my coat and backpack down on the floor in the front hall. "Sorry I'm late," I called. I struggled to catch my breath.

"Where were you? You missed dinner." Mom stepped into the hall, hands on her hips. "We called Mrs Lange. She said you left on time."

"Are you angry or worried?" I asked.

"Both."

"It's no big deal," I said. "I'm fine. Really. I can explain, OK? Just give me one minute."

I didn't wait for her answer. I turned and grabbed the door to the basement stairs.

I could hear Mom and Dad shouting after me. But I hurtled down to the basement, taking the stairs two at a time.

I had to make sure the mask was locked tightly in its box. *No way* I could let it escape on Halloween. The man in the mask store was wrong. He *had* to be wrong!

I grabbed the string and pulled on the ceiling bulb in the storage room. I began shoving cartons out of the way. My whole body was shaking as I uncovered the metal box.

I was gasping for breath. My throat ached and my hands trembled. Somehow, I managed to unlock the box.

I pulled open the lid – and SCREAMED.

"What IS this? What IS this?" I cried.

I tugged out the white and yellow feathers. My *duck costume*! The awful duck costume my mom made for me. Stuffed into the box.

I pulled it out and tossed it to the floor. And stared . . . stared into the empty box.

The Haunted Mask was GONE!

18

I stared into the empty box, my mind spinning. I bent and picked up the feathery duck costume. I shook it hard. Was the mask hiding inside?

No.

I slumped down on to a carton to think. A million questions flashed through my mind. All of them were terrifying.

How did this happen? Did the mask escape? Did the man in the mask store tell the truth?

He said someone else wanted it. Did someone come into my house and steal it?

How did they know where it was hidden?

Whoa. Hold on a minute.

I suddenly remembered something. Noah had been down in the basement. Did he see me with the mask? Was he down here that night I left the box uncovered?

I suddenly had a heavy feeling in the pit of my stomach. I felt sick.

Switching the mask for the duck costume was the kind of joke Noah liked to pull. If he took the mask up to his room, he had to try it on. No way he could resist.

Was he stuck inside the mask right now, controlled by its evil?

My heart was pounding like crazy. I forced myself to my feet. And ran up the stairs.

Mom called to me from the kitchen. "Carly Beth, do you want your dinner now? Are you OK?"

"In a minute!" I shouted. I flew up the stairs. I ran down the hall to Noah's room. "Noah?" I called. "Noah? Are you all right?"

I threw open his door – and gasped.

Slowly, Noah turned around. And his eyes stared out at me through his craggy green mask.

19

I staggered back against the wall.

Inside the mask, Noah blinked at me. "What's your problem, weirdo? I'm trying on my new Hulk mask. You've never seen the Incredible Hulk before?"

I stared at the bumpy green mask. And burst out laughing. "You look awesome, Noah," I said. "I just wasn't expecting. . ."

"I wanted to be Wolverine," he said. His voice was muffled behind the rubber mask. "But they only had the Hulk."

"Well, I think it's an improvement," I said. "You should keep it on."

He kicked me in the leg.

"Don't get violent," I said.

"Are you joking? You're telling the Hulk not to get violent?"

He let out a roar and tackled me around the waist. We both fell to the floor, laughing. Roaring some more, he tried to pin my arms to the rug.

"Carly Beth? What's going on up there?" Mom shouted from the bottom of the stairs. "I'm getting really angry. Are you coming down for your dinner or what?"

"Coming!" I called, pushing the Incredible Hulk off me. "Be right down!"

I checked my room. I just wanted to make sure the Haunted Mask wasn't hiding there, waiting for me.

Then I hurried down for dinner.

I didn't have much of an appetite. I was too stressed. I knew I'd be seeing that mask again soon.

And what would I do when I saw it?

What would I do?

20

On Halloween night, Sabrina and I jogged up the gravel path to the farmhouse. We were both dressed as clowns. We had painted our faces white. We wore ruffly pink clown collars around our necks. And red rubber clown noses pinched on to our faces.

Bright yellow light poured from all the windows. I could hear shouts and music and kids laughing.

We pulled open the front door, and Laura came hurrying over to us. She was wearing a silvery princess dress. Her face was red and her hair was wild around her face.

"Get in here!" she cried breathlessly. She pulled me in by my coat. "I'm so glad to see you. Where have you been?"

"We waited an hour for the bus," I said. "I'm so sorry we're late."

Laura sighed. "I'm sorry, too," she said. "The kids are totally wild tonight. They're all going ballistic. It's like I have eight Jesses!"

"We'll try to calm them down," Sabrina said.

"Look at my princess costume," Laura said. She pointed to the front of her skirt. "Angela spat up orange juice on my dress."

"Angela the perfect angel?" I said.

"Angela isn't an angel tonight," Laura grumbled.

Sabrina and I tossed off our coats and followed Laura into the playroom. We had strung orange and black streamers over the walls and ceiling.

I saw Jesse pulling streamers down. He carried a long black streamer over to Colin and used it to tie Colin's hands behind his back.

Colin struggled to free himself and knocked over a plate of cookies. The two boys started wrestling on the floor.

Two other boys were popping the orange and black balloons that had been strung up. Debra was hunched in the corner, wailing. "I want to go home! I don't LIKE Halloween!"

"Looks like a good party," Sabrina joked.

Laura rolled her eyes. "Let's split up," she said. "We're outnumbered, but we can handle them."

It took a while to get them sitting down. Then Laura taught them a spooky Halloween song I'd never heard before. It had a lot of creepy *OOOOOH OOOOOH OOOOH*s in it, which the kids loved.

Then I suggested the kids make up their own scary ghost story. But they started *Ooooh oooh ooohing* around the room. And Jesse found some

Gummi Worms, which he tried to stuff down the back of Harmony's witch costume.

"I was planning to show them how to carve a jack-o'-lantern," Laura said. "But *no way* I'm taking out any knives with this group tonight!"

"They're totally wired," I said. "But they've been eating Halloween candy all day."

Another balloon popped. Debra started crying again.

That's when Mrs Lange swept into the room. She wore a witch's costume with a long black dress and pointed black hat. She had a black mask pulled down over her eyes and carried an old-fashioned straw broom.

She tossed back her head and cackled. A pretty good witch's cackle. It got the kids' attention.

"Let's pick up these spilled cookies," she said, pointing to the floor. "Or else I'll put a spell on y'all and turn you into disgusting *spiders*!" She cackled again.

Several kids dived to the floor and started to collect the spilled cookies.

"Laura, didn't you want to help these children make their own masks?" Mrs Lange said. She started to carry art supplies to the table. "Let's get started. They can make masks out of these paper bags. I want to see the scariest masks ever!"

The kids didn't pay much attention to her. They were running around the room, pulling down streamers, tossing apples at each other, looking for Halloween candy.

I let out a sigh. I thought this would be a fun way to celebrate Halloween. But the kids weren't cooperating. And I couldn't really concentrate anyway.

I kept gazing around the room. How could I enjoy the Halloween party? I couldn't get the Haunted Mask out of my mind.

"Carly Beth?"

It took me a few moments to realize Mrs Lange was calling me. I shook my head hard, shaking away my scary thoughts. "Yes?"

"Would you go to my office?" Mrs Lange asked. "I left a box of markers on my desk. They'll be perfect for mask making."

"No problem," I said. I left the playroom and made my way down the long front hall. My shoes clunked on the hardwood floors.

I passed a music room with an old piano pushed against one wall. Then a small bedroom with a painting of racing horses above the bed.

Mrs Lange's office was the last room at the end. I stepped inside and clicked on the ceiling light.

The window was open. The pale yellow curtains fluttered into the room like ghosts.

Her computer was on, a photo of a grinning Labrador retriever on the monitor. Her desk was piled high with magazines and papers and a tall stack of books.

I bent over the desk, searching for the box of markers.

A book in the corner caught my eye. It was an old book with a ragged grey cover. Its title was *Tumbledown Times*.

I picked it up. It smelled musty. I opened it and saw that it was a history of Tumbledown Farms. I thumbed through it quickly – and stopped at a section of old photos in the middle.

The first faded black-and-white photo was of the original farmhouse. Just a little wooden shack. The next photo showed some grinning farm-workers holding shovels and pitchforks in front of a hay wagon.

I blinked when I turned the page and saw the next old photo. The stable. I recognized it immediately. Two tall horses stood at the side, heads lowered.

And leaning against the doorway was the stable boy. He had a long piece of straw in his mouth.

I raised the book closer, staring at the stable boy.

He looked familiar.

Yes! I squinted at the picture till I could see the face clearly.

And then my breath caught in my throat. And I suddenly felt cold all over.

The stable boy was CLARK!

21

Clark is a ghost.

I held the book in my trembling hands and stared at the boy's face. Yes. It was definitely Clark.

Clark is a ghost.

I slammed the book shut and dropped it to the desk. I remembered the words of the man from the mask store. *"Someone else is out there. Someone else who owned the mask and will do anything to get it back."* It was Clark! "I have to tell Sabrina," I said out loud.

I picked up the box of markers and went running out of the room. I lurched down the long hall, my heart pounding. I burst into the playroom and shouted, "Sabrina? Sabrina?"

I stopped when I saw Clark. He was standing against the glass door at the back. His hair fell down over his forehead. His hands were at his sides.

"Oh!" I let out a startled cry. Panic tightened in my throat.

Clark, what are you doing here? I thought. *I know the truth about you. I know you were the stable boy. I know you are a ghost.*

Why are you here?

Clark stepped away from the door. He said something to Angela and Colin. Then he reached behind his back – and pulled something from his pocket.

A *mask*!

The mask that had panicked the horses. MY HAUNTED MASK?

Clark pulled the rubber mask down over his face. An ugly mask. But not my mask. It was green and big-eyed and had a long alligator snout with two rows of pointy yellow teeth.

He fixed it over his head and stepped towards the kids.

"NOOOOO!" I wanted to scream for him to stop. But no sound came out.

I knew I had to act fast. Clark was a ghost, and I was the only one who knew it. The kids weren't safe. *None* of us were safe.

I grabbed Sabrina and spun her around. "Quick—" I choked out. "Take the kids to the art table. Keep them close together. Make masks with them."

"Mrs Lange and I tried," Sabrina said. "They wouldn't sit down."

"Listen to me!" I screamed. "Get them away from Clark. Sit them down and make the masks over there." I pointed to the art table on the other side of the room.

"Hel-lo?" Sabrina said. "Carly Beth? Why are you so freaked?"

"Tell you later," I said, my eyes on Clark in that hideous mask. "Where is Mrs Lange?"

"She and Laura had to go out to get more apple juice," Sabrina said. She studied me for a minute. She could see how frightened I was.

"OK. I – I'll round up the kids." She turned and started to herd the kids to the art table.

I helped push Jesse and Debra in the right direction. "Come over here," I said, trying to sound calm. I didn't want to scare the kids. "Take a paper bag. Let's make some scary Halloween masks. The creepier the better!"

Once the kids were settled, I took a deep breath and strode across the room to Clark.

"Carly Beth – hi," he said. His voice was muffled inside the ugly mask. His dark eyes locked on mine.

"I know the truth," I said. "I . . . I know the truth about you, Clark." I grabbed the top of his mask with both hands – and tugged it off his head.

"Hey!!" He cried out angrily. He grabbed for the mask. "What is your *problem*?"

I studied his face. Yes. I wasn't making a mistake.

My heart pounded. I struggled to breathe. I was standing so close to a *ghost*!

"You were the stable boy," I said. "You're the one who killed those horses all those years ago. I saw your picture in an old book. I know it was you, Clark. I know what you are. You're a *ghost*."

His eyes didn't move off me. But his smile faded. "Yes, you're right, Carly Beth," he said softly. "Now you know the truth."

22

I staggered back.

He lurched forward and brought his face close to mine. "I'm going to put this mask back on – and destroy everyone in this room!" he whispered.

"No—" I gasped. I swung the ugly mask behind my back and gripped it tightly with both hands.

And then Clark laughed. He shook his head and laughed hard.

"Carly Beth, are you totally nuts?" he cried. "I'm just kidding around. That was a *joke*."

"Not a joke," I insisted. "I saw you in that old photo in the book about Tumbledown Farms. I studied the photo carefully. I—"

"I've seen that old photo, too," Clark said. "It's my grandfather. My grandfather was the stable boy. He was about my age then. And I look a lot like him."

"You're lying," I said. "The stable boy died in

that stampede. So he *couldn't* be your grandfather! It's *you* in that photo! I know it!"

I glanced back at the table. The kids were already finishing their masks. Some were cutting eye holes into the paper bags.

Clark pulled his mask away from me, then held it up to my face. "Check it out, Carly Beth. It's just an alligator. It's a normal Halloween mask. I bought it at the supermarket. It's not the evil mask that frightened the horses."

I couldn't stop shaking. I didn't believe him. "Clark, photos don't lie," I said. "You were the stable boy. Why are you here? Are you looking for the Haunted Mask? Is that why you came tonight?"

He blinked. "Huh? Haunted Mask? No. I—"

I glanced back. The kids were trying on their masks. Pulling the brown paper bags over their heads.

"I don't know what you want," I told Clark. "I don't know why you're haunting this farm. But please – don't harm the kids."

Clark's mouth dropped open. "You're crazy!" he said. "You're totally crazy! Listen to me—"

Before he could finish, I heard the first scream from the kids' table.

"HELP ME!"

I spun around – and saw the kids with their paper bag masks pulled down over their heads.

85

"Help me! I can't get it off!" Colin screamed. He was tugging at the top of the mask.

Two or three other kids began pulling at their masks and screaming.

"It's STUCK to me!"

"It won't come off!"

"It hurts! It HURTS! Take it off!"

A cry of horror escaped my throat. The kids were trapped in their masks – just as I had been.

Clark did this to them. But why? To teach me a *lesson*?

I tossed his alligator mask across the room and hurried to the table to help the kids. They were screaming and crying, pulling and scratching wildly at the paper bag masks. I could see the masks tightening around the kids' faces.

"Clark! Stop it!" I screamed. "Let the kids alone! Stop doing this!"

"HELP ME, CARLY BETH! IT HURTS! IT HURTS!" Harmony wailed.

"OW! I CAN'T SEE! I CAN'T BREATHE!" Jesse cried.

"Clark – what do you want?" I said. "Stop this – *please*!"

He stood right behind me. I grabbed his arm. "Hey!"

He was solid. His arm was warm.

I gasped. "Y-you're alive!" I cried. "You're alive. You're not a ghost."

My head spun. I suddenly felt so confused.

86

The kids were all on their feet, screaming and pulling frantically at their masks. I grabbed the bottom of Jesse's mask and tried to tear it off. But it stuck tightly to his neck and shoulders.

Beside me, Sabrina held Debra by one shoulder. She tried to tug off Debra's mask. She gave a hard pull. But the mask didn't budge. Debra let out a loud, horrified wail, her little hands flying in the air.

The door swung open. Laura burst in. Her blonde hair flew around her face. Her eyes moved from kid to kid.

She strode over to Clark and me. She had a strange, wild expression on her face. Was she *smiling*?

"Sorry I had to scare the kids like this," Laura said.

"Huh?" I gaped at her, at her cold silvery eyes.

"It was the only way to get you to cooperate, Carly Beth," Laura said. "Do you want to save these kids? There's only one way."

"Laura – I don't understand," I stammered. "What are you talking about?"

"BRING ME THE HAUNTED MASK!" she screamed. "I cannot rest until it is MINE again! Bring it, Carly Beth – and you'd better hurry!"

23

I staggered back until I hit the wall. The lights suddenly seemed too bright. The floor felt unsteady beneath my feet.

I saw the startled look on Clark's face. And I saw Sabrina hugging herself, trembling in fright.

The kids were running in crazy circles around the room. Screaming and crying, they tugged and slapped at their masks.

"Get the massssk!" Laura hissed at me. "I need it, Carly Beth. I've been waiting so many years. Sooooo many years. Waiting to have it again."

I fought back my fear. I glared at her. "*You're* the ghost!" I cried.

She pushed back her wild hair. Her eyes flashed. "Yes, yesssssss. It was me. All me. It wasn't the stable boy. Clark's grandfather. He didn't wear the mask. I did! *I'm* the one who died in that stampede!"

She floated off the floor. "I can't ressssst until I have the mask again," she said. She had to scream over the cries of the kids. Her weird silver eyes burned down at me.

"My father owned Tumbledown Farms. And I destroyed it all. I wore the mask as a joke. To scare the stable boy. I didn't know the mask was evil. I didn't know its evil would change me for ever!"

She lowered herself to the floor. I could feel a wave of cold off her body.

"I've been waiting here at the farm for sooooo long," Laura continued. "The other night, I heard you at the stable, Carly Beth. I heard you talking to Clark. I heard you tell him you had the Haunted Mask. And I knew my long wait was finally over."

"Laura – let the kids go!" I shouted. "Let them take off their masks!"

"Nooooo!" she replied, rising over me. Her long hair flew up at the sides of her head like wings. "Bring me the mask first! I can't go to my final rest until I have the mask. Don't stand there! Go get it! Before the kids start to suffocate!"

My breath caught in my throat. I suddenly remembered. I suddenly remembered opening the metal box in my basement. Pulling out that feathery costume.

"Laura – I don't have the Haunted Mask!" I cried.

"LIAR!" she screamed. Her eyes flamed bright red with rage. "LIAR! Go get it – NOW!"

89

"But . . . it's *gone*!" I told her. "I don't have it. I'm telling the truth! It . . . it disappeared!"

Laura floated above me. Her fists were tight. She swung them in the air. Her eyes still flamed bright red.

"Do you want these kids to suffocate in their masks because you are a LIAR?"

"You've *got* to believe me!" I begged. "The mask is *gone*!"

And then I heard a tiny voice from the corner. Sabrina's voice. "I know where it is," she said.

24

The kids were screaming and crying. They ran in circles around us, tugging at their paper masks.

Sabrina took a timid step closer. I stared at her in shock.

Laura floated to the floor. She lowered her fists and turned her angry red stare on Sabrina.

"I was only trying to help you, Carly Beth," Sabrina said in a frightened whisper. "I sneaked into your house and took the mask from your basement. I knew you weren't safe with the mask in your house. I . . . buried it outside the stable. No one ever goes there."

So *that* was the patch of freshly dug earth. I thought it was a grave.

"Get it *now*," Laura ordered. "Dig it up. Bring it to me. Or I'll make these kids suffer even more."

"You can't get away with this!" Clark roared.

I jumped back as he leaped into the air. He reached out both arms to tackle Laura to the floor.

But Clark's hands went right *through* her! A ghost. You can't tackle a ghost!

She rose off the floor. She pointed a long finger at him and gave him a cold, hard stare.

"NOOOO!" Clark let out a startled scream as she held him in her stare. And he went sailing backwards across the room.

CRAAAAACK! His head slammed into the wall with a hard jolt. He uttered a groan and then slumped in a heap to the floor.

With a cold smile on her face, Laura turned to me. "See what I can do?" she said. "Would you like to see the kids go flying head first?"

She waved me to the door. "Stop stalling, Carly Beth. You know you have no choice. Go dig it up. Bring me the Haunted Mask."

She was right. I had no choice. I ran out the glass door, with the kids' wails and shrieks of pain ringing in my ears.

A blast of cold wind pushed me back. Hugging myself, I lowered my head and ran across the garden towards the stable.

My breath steamed up in front of me. My shoes crunched on the frosty hard ground.

The tall grass blew from side to side. Pale silver moonlight made a path in front of me as I ran.

The lighted path disappeared as I stepped into the darkness of the apple orchard. I hurtled through the blur of tree limbs and branches and dark trunks trying to block my way.

My side throbbed with pain and my dry throat ached as I reached the stable. I found the patch where Sabrina had buried the mask. I didn't wait to catch my breath. I dropped to my knees and began to heave up earth with both hands.

It didn't take long. Sabrina hadn't buried it very deep. I pulled it up from its shallow grave. The mask felt WARM!

I shook the earth off it. It stared up at me as I held it in my trembling hands.

I raced through the orchard to the farmhouse. Would I be in time to save those poor kids? *Could* I save them? Would Laura really release them from their masks?

Shivering from the cold, I stepped through the front door. I held the mask in front of me.

The kids were quiet now. Their screams had stopped. Some were lying on the floor, weakly tugging at their masks. A few were huddled together in a corner, crying softly.

Laura rushed forward to meet me. Her eyes gleamed when they landed on the mask. "Give it to me!" she cried. "I've waited so long! I need it!"

Breathing hard, my whole body shivered. I started to hand it to her.

She reached for it. Her pale eyes flashed with excitement.

I pulled it back.

The mask will make Laura even more evil, I thought. *She doesn't want it back so she can finally go to her resting place.*

She waited for the mask all this time so she could do more EVIL!

If she gets the mask, she will destroy us all!

"Give it," Laura whispered. She made a wild grab for it. "Give it to me, Carly Beth."

I could feel her ghostly powers, so strong and cold. I could feel the pull. Feel her pulling my arm . . . pulling the mask to her.

"No!" I choked out.

I made a terrifying decision. Someone had to save the kids.

I gripped the Haunted Mask by its sides. I raised it high.

And I pulled it down over *my own head*!

I gasped. The warmth of the mask burned my face. I could feel the mask instantly start to tighten.

But I knew I had to fight evil with evil.

I heard the children screaming. I turned and saw them tearing off their paper bag masks. Their faces were red and drenched with sweat. But they were laughing and crying and jumping up and down with joy.

All of Laura's attention was on me. She had released her hold on the kids.

Mrs Lange ran in. "What's all the screaming?" she asked. "I had a problem in the office. I—"

Her face went pale. She saw Laura and me facing each other. She saw me in the Haunted Mask. Her whole body shuddered. Without another word, she gathered up the kids and hurried them out of the farmhouse.

Laura's flaming eyes were locked on mine. "You FOOL!" she screamed. "Take it OFF! Give it to me!"

I could feel the mask shrinking against my skin. Attaching itself to my head. And I could feel its evil pouring down me, like ice water filling my body.

"You FOOL!" Laura shouted again. "I wanted to DESTROY the mask! I didn't want to *wear* it!"

"Liar!" I cried. My voice came out raspy and deep behind the mask. I knew she was lying.

With a cry, Laura leaped forward and grabbed the mask with both hands. "Give it to me! It's mine! It's MINE! You'll PAY! I'll make you PAY!"

She tugged at the cheeks. Then raised her hands to the top of the mask and pulled.

"No! Let go! Let GO!" I screamed. The mask was stuck to me. It was part of me. The ugly mask was now my FACE!

I could feel the hot anger burn my chest. I couldn't control my rage.

I let out a furious roar. I wasn't me any more. I was some kind of *beast.* "You're DOOMED, Laura! Tonight you face your doom!"

Grunting like an animal, I lunged at her. I made a grab for her. Missed. My hands pushed right through her.

"You can't escape me, Laura!" I roared.

I saw a flash of fear on her ghostly face. She swung away and ran out the glass door to the back.

I saw her running across the garden, and I took off after her.

Into the cold, windy darkness. My shoes pounded hard over the frosty ground. The tall grass flattened as I plunged through it.

"You can't escape, Laura!" I growled.

She floated over the pasture, her hair flying behind her. I raced after her, arms outstretched.

Silence fell over us. A deep, frightening silence.

And then, running hard, I tilted my head back – and roared out a shrill cry.

Not a cry from me. Not a cry from Carly Beth.

The cry came from the mask. It was the scream of the Haunted Mask.

The mask had taken over my mind and my body.

The mask had *won*!

26

My scream rang out over the empty pasture. It was an animal cry – not human. A scream of pure anger and raging evil.

I screamed again and again and felt the mask burn itself to my skin. I screamed as I ran – and then the scream stopped with a gasp of surprise.

I heard a rumbling sound. Panting like an animal, I listened. And heard the whinny of horses. And the soft thunder of hoofbeats.

And then a dozen ghostly horses came galloping out from the blackness of the orchard trees. Pale, pale horses. Their white manes flew behind their raised heads. Their eyes glowed an icy blue. Their mouths were open as if in a permanent cry.

The ground shook. The tall pasture grass whipped in all directions. The ghost horses galloped together. They held their heads tall and high. Their glowing blue eyes were trained on Laura.

Laura uttered a cry. She couldn't escape.

The horses swirled around her, galloping faster and faster. I stared in amazement as they became a cloud of white. A loud, frightening blur of ghostly blue eyes and whinnies and screams and pounding hoofbeats.

And then the cloud faded. The horses slowed and pulled away from their whirling circle.

Silence now. A heavy, hushed silence. The grass stopped its wild dance. The wind didn't blow.

No more screams. Laura was gone. Vanished in the ghostly stampede.

I watched the horses turn back towards the orchard. They lowered their heads and grunted softly to one another. They could relax now. The girl who had frightened them so many years ago was finally gone.

I waited until the horses had disappeared into the trees. Then I turned and strode back to the house.

Sabrina and Clark came rushing across the garden to greet me. But they stopped when they saw my ugly green rutted face. I heard them gasp when they saw the glow of evil in my eyes.

"Oh! Carly Beth!" Sabrina shouted.

I picked up the wheelbarrow in the middle of the garden. Hoisted it high over my head – and *heaved* it against the back door. I raised my face to the sky and laughed as the glass shattered.

"Go away – both of you!" I roared. "I'm not Carly Beth any more! I AM the Haunted Mask!"

"No! Carly Beth – we can help you!" Clark cried.

But I picked up a garden hoe. Pulled back my arm. And tossed it at his head.

"Nooo!" Clark and Sabrina screamed. Clark ducked, and the hoe sailed over him.

I searched for something else to throw. Clark and Sabrina turned and darted back into the house.

I raised my head and howled at the moon.

I couldn't control my anger. I wanted to pull down the trees and tear the farmhouse apart board by board.

I dropped to my knees. *Am I doomed to be like this for ever? To act and look like this?* I asked myself. *Is there no cure for me?*

I remembered that first Halloween. I remembered what the store owner told me about the mask.

"It can be removed only by a symbol of love."

I gazed around. "There *is* no love here," I muttered. "There is only fear and anger. Besides, the store owner said the mask could be removed only *once* by a symbol of love."

But I'd defeated the mask then. I'd *survived*. The store owner said I was the only one. . . He said he didn't know what would happen. . .

On my knees on the frozen ground, I screamed

100

at the moon once more. I screamed long and hard. When I lowered my head, I saw the horses returning. Stampeding over the tall grass. Once again, their ghostly white manes flew, and their eyes glowed an icy blue.

Galloping straight at me. Coming for ME now!

I shut my eyes. Gritted my teeth.

And prepared for the pain.

27

Kneeling on the ground, I listened to the thunder of hoofbeats. I steadied myself . . . steadied myself . . . and felt a tingle on my cheek.

I opened my eyes. A horse nuzzled my cheek. Another ghostly pale horse lowered its head and nudged me. It wanted to be petted.

The horses formed a close circle around me, whinnying softly, bumping me gently.

I wrapped my arms around a horse's neck.

And from some faraway place, I heard a soft voice. Laura's voice. "Carly Beth, you were the only one to care for them in all these years," she called to me. "The only one to show them any love."

It took me a long moment to realize what Laura was talking about.

The carrots!

I'd brought them carrots – a symbol of kindness and love.

My heart pounding. I climbed to my feet. And

with a cry of joy, I *ripped* off the Haunted Mask. Yes! It came off! It came off!

The cool air greeted my burning face. Slowly, the anger and rage floated away. I could feel the mask release its hold on my mind.

The horses quickly began to fade. They vanished except for their glowing blue eyes. The eyes floated above me, shimmering against the black sky like stars. And then they vanished, too.

I turned and saw Sabrina and Clark standing outside the back door. I ran to them and threw my arms around Sabrina in a hug.

"Sabrina, I can't stop shaking," I said. "But I'm so *happy*! The nightmare is over. For everyone. It's finally *over*!"

I glanced down. I suddenly realized I still had the Haunted Mask gripped tightly in my hand.

I raised it in front of me. I turned to Sabrina and Clark. "We have to bury it again," I said. "Right away. We—"

I stopped when the mask wiggled in my hand. The ugly green head started to quiver and shake. The fat rubbery lips began to move up and down. And to my horror, I heard its whispered rasp:

"You're my favourite, Carly Beth. See you next Halloween. . ."

ENTER
HORRORLAND

THE STORY SO FAR. . .

Ordinary kids are receiving mysterious invitations to HorrorLand, a popular SCREAM park filled with ghoulish rides and attractions. Each "very special guest" is promised a week of scary fun — but now the scares are becoming a little TOO scary.

Two girls — Britney Crosby and Molly Molloy — disappeared in the Black Lagoon Water Park, and Billy Deep was horrified when his sister, Sheena, suddenly became invisible. Then, she went missing, too.

A park guide — a Horror named Byron — warned the kids they were all in danger. He tried to help them . . . until two other Horrors dragged him away!

Why are the kids in danger? Where are the three missing girls? Maybe Byron knows the answers — if the kids can find him.

When Carly Beth and Sabrina received invitations of their own, they had no idea they might be stepping into a REAL horror story!

What's next? Turn the page to join Carly Beth and Sabrina in HorrorLand. . .

1

Nothing can scare me. Not after my horrifying battles with the Haunted Mask.

So when the envelope addressed to Carly Beth Caldwell arrived in the mail from HorrorLand Amusement Park, I wasn't afraid at all. I knew I would have a great time there – even though everyone says HorrorLand is the scariest place on earth.

The invitation said I could bring a friend to the park for a week – absolutely free! So when summer arrived, I was ready to put the *real* scares behind me. And enjoy some *fun* scares for a change.

Our first day at the park, Sabrina and I took our seats in the Very Special Guests section of the Haunted Theatre. Creepy organ music played. Shadow ghosts slid across the purple curtain onstage. Evil laughter poured out of hidden speakers.

"This is totally awesome," Sabrina said. "How did you ever get picked to come here for free?"

I shrugged. "Beats me. No idea."

A deep voice came over the speakers. "Attention, everyone. Mondo the Magical is backstage casting a spell on himself. Unfortunately, he turned himself into a pigeon. The show will begin as soon as he turns himself back."

Everyone laughed. I gazed around. The theatre was about half full. Kids and families were still pouring in.

The room was long and narrow, with rows of ghost-white seats. Photos of screaming faces lined the purple walls.

Sabrina bumped me with her elbow. "Look. Those two boys are going to sit with us."

I turned to the aisle and saw a Horror – that's what they call the park guides here. He was dressed in green and purple, and he was showing two boys to the chairs next to us.

Sabrina smoothed down her hair and adjusted her pale green T-shirt. "They're kind of cute," she whispered.

The boys dropped into their seats. They both had dark hair and dark eyes. Sabrina leaned forward to say hi. But they totally ignored us. They seemed to be stressed about something.

"Billy, I saw them drag Byron into this theatre,"

the taller one said. "I'll bet they are holding him backstage."

Billy's face was red. He kept glancing at the Horror ushers in the aisle. "Stay cool, Matt," he whispered. "Just act as if we're here to see the show. Maybe when the lights go down, we can sneak out and search for Byron."

I stared at them. What was their *problem*?

"But maybe we should search for Sheena, Britney and Molly first," the one named Billy said.

Matt shook his head. "Don't you get it? Byron said he would help us. He knows what's going on. We've got to rescue him from those Horrors who dragged him away."

Billy slammed his hands on the arms of the seat. "Where is my sister? How can this be happening?"

Matt had something in his hand. I squinted to see it better. It was a tiny piece of a mirror. The two boys sat there, staring into it.

OK. I'm not a nosy person. But this was too much.

"What's up with you guys?" I asked. "What are you looking at?"

Their heads shot around. "Oh. Hi," Matt said.

"Didn't see you," Billy said.

"What's up?" I asked again. "You both look totally stressed."

They glanced at each other. They were trying to decide whether to tell me or not.

"Well . . . we have a weird problem," Billy said finally. "My sister, Sheena, is missing. And two other girls we met."

Sabrina's mouth dropped open. "Missing? For real? Did you tell the park people about it?"

Billy rolled his eyes. "Like they want to be helpful?"

"A Horror named Byron wants to help us," Matt said. "But some other Horrors dragged him away."

Matt saw me gazing at the mirror. He held it up to me. "What do you see in there?"

I pulled the tiny piece of mirror closer. "I see two girls on some kind of carnival ride," I said.

"Those are the two missing girls," Matt said. "Britney and Molly."

I studied the girls in the mirror. "What is it? Some kind of optical illusion?"

"No. It's real," Billy said. "We have to find that carousel. Maybe my sister is there with them. But she may be a little hard to find. She's invisible."

I glanced at Sabrina. She looked as confused as I did. Their story didn't make any sense at all. Missing girls inside a mirror? An invisible girl? They seemed too upset to be joking. But could it be *true*?

Matt turned to me. He was very good-looking. Billy was skinny, but Matt looked like he played sports. "Are you special guests, too? Did you get free invitations?" he asked.

"Yes," I said.

"We had scary things happen to us before we got here," Matt said. "Billy and his sister had to fight a bunch of zombie pirates. And I had some problems with this terrible stuff called Monster Blood."

I pictured the Haunted Mask and my temples began to pound.

"We think they invited us to this park because of the scary things that happened to us this year," Billy said. "Did something scary happen to you?"

Should I tell them? I don't even know them.

I decided I'd better not.

"Uh . . . no way," I answered. "Nothing scary ever happened to me."

Sabrina poked me and started to say something. But I gave her a look that made her stay quiet.

The theatre lights faded. A bright yellow spotlight shone down on the curtain onstage. Music blared from the speakers. The show was starting.

Matt climbed to his feet and crouched down. He tapped Billy's shoulder. "Come on. They're not watching," he whispered. "Let's go look for Byron."

He glared at me. "Wish us luck," he whispered. "We'll need it."

The two boys began creeping to the aisle.

113

Two Horrors quickly moved to block the aisle. The boys had no choice. They sank back into their seats. They stared straight ahead at the stage. I could see they were really upset.

Mondo the Magical strutted onstage. He was a chubby little man with a shiny bald head and a big crooked nose. He wore a tight-fitting tuxedo with a big red bow tie and had a long purple cape draped over his back.

He took a deep bow. Everyone clapped. He held an egg in his hand. Waved it around in a circle. And it disappeared.

Then he pulled two eggs from his ear. He waved them around, and suddenly, he held four eggs. He waved the four eggs, and they all disappeared.

Sabrina leaned close to me. "Pretty lame," she whispered.

"You'll like this one better," Mondo announced.

Sabrina and I gasped. How did he hear that?

Mondo's assistant was a young woman with long blonde hair and bright red lips. She wore a glittery costume of reds and yellows. She wheeled a steaming cauldron onstage.

Mondo waved his hands over the cauldron. He formed one hand into a cup. And then he pulled a live rabbit out of his fist!

Sabrina and I clapped. That was a pretty good trick. Billy and Matt stared straight ahead. I could tell they weren't thinking about the magic act.

"Here is a trick that only Mondo can do!" Mondo announced. "A trick no other magician has even dreamed of!"

He lifted the bunny rabbit in the palm of one hand. Then he appeared to reach his other hand down the rabbit's mouth. And he pulled a hat out of the rabbit!

I laughed hard. What a funny idea, pulling a hat out of a rabbit. Yes, that *had* to be a first.

Mondo took another deep bow. When he stood up, his eyes bulged. He grabbed his throat and began to make loud choking sounds.

Some kids gasped. The audience grew very silent.

Mondo reached two fingers into his mouth – and pulled out a ping-pong ball. He made more choking sounds. He pulled out another ping-pong ball. Then another. And another.

Pretty soon, a dozen ping-pong balls bounced across the stage, all pulled from Mondo's mouth.

"Mondo has a big mouth," he said. "Anyone like to play tennis?" He opened his mouth wide and pulled out a tennis ball.

Sabrina poked me. "He's pulling them from his sleeve," she whispered.

"Here's one you won't be able to figure out!" Mondo boomed.

Could he hear Sabrina's whisper?

The assistant rolled a tall box onstage. It looked like a coffin standing on end.

"Say goodbye to my assistant, Rhonda," Mondo said. "She is going to disappear *for ever*!"

Mondo pulled open the lid. Then he banged the four sides of the box with his cane. "Solid wood," he said.

He pointed for his assistant to get into the box. "Goodbye, Rhonda," he said. "It's been great!"

Rhonda waved goodbye to the audience. Then she tossed back her long blonde hair and stepped into the box. Mondo blew her a kiss. Then he closed the lid.

"We'll never see Rhonda again," Mondo said. "Who wants to be my new assistant? I need a new assistant every day!"

He pulled out a yellow blanket and wrapped it around the box. "Everyone count with me!" he said. He led the count: "One . . . two . . . THREE!"

He pulled the blanket off the box and tossed it away. Then he grabbed the handle – and tugged the lid open.

"Empty!" he cried.

A big puff of black smoke.

As the smoke cleared, Mondo let out a startled gasp.

A dark-haired girl stood in the box. She wore a pale blue T-shirt and faded jeans. She kept blinking and shaking her head.

She stepped out of the box.

A hush fell over the theatre.

And then I saw Billy jump to his feet. "My *sister*!" he gasped. "SHEENA!"

3

"I . . . I don't understand," Mondo muttered. He wiped sweat off his bald head and gaped at the girl. "How did you—? I mean – where?"

Was this part of the act? I didn't think so. He gazed out into the audience. He looked as if he suddenly remembered we were there. "Thank you! Thank you!" he cried. Then he ran off the stage without taking a bow.

All the theatre doors swung open, and everyone left. I watched Billy and Matt run on to the stage to greet Sheena. Billy actually *hugged* his sister! "You're back! I can see you!" he said.

I started to the exit. There were a *million* things I wanted to do in the park. But Sabrina pulled me to the stage. "We have to see what's up with these kids," she said.

Sheena still looked a little unsteady and confused. Matt stood there staring at her as if she was a ghost or something.

And Billy started tossing question after question

at the poor girl: "Where were you? Do you know where you were? Did you see Britney and Molly? Were they OK? Did you talk to them? How did you get back?"

Sheena sat down on the edge of the stage. She kept twirling a strand of her dark hair between her fingers. "It's . . . hard to remember everything," she said softly.

"Well, *try*!" Billy insisted. He and Matt dropped down beside her. Sabrina and I stayed near the first row of seats.

"At first, everything was green," Sheena said. "Like a thick green fog. Then I realized it was the Monster Blood. Remember? I got vacuumed up with all that Monster Blood?"

I turned to Sabrina. "Monster Blood?" I whispered. "What's going on here?"

"I was covered in that sticky goo," Sheena continued. "I . . . pulled it away from my eyes. And finally I could see clearly."

"Where were you?" Billy demanded.

"In some other part of HorrorLand, I think," Sheena replied. "Some part we haven't seen. I looked all around. I didn't recognize anything."

"What did you see?" Matt asked.

"There was a strange carousel," Sheena said. "The carousel horses were on fire. They didn't burn. But they had flames shooting out of them."

Billy turned to Matt, very excited. "The same carousel we saw in the mirror!" he cried.

"Sheena," Matt said, "did you see Britney and Molly riding the burning carousel?"

She nodded. "Yes. I saw them. I waved to them. And they waved back."

"Did you talk to them?" Matt asked.

Sheena shook her head. "I couldn't get close enough," she said. "I started running to them. But I couldn't get any closer. I ran and ran. But the carousel stayed just as far away from me. It was unreal – like being in a dream."

"Then what happened?" Matt asked.

"A door opened in front of me. It appeared out of nowhere," Sheena said. "I stepped through it. And here I was. Back!"

I turned to Sabrina. "She has to be making this up," I whispered. "It's some kind of scary HorrorLand joke – right?"

But the two boys weren't laughing. "We've got to search the park and find that carousel," Matt said. He pulled Sheena to her feet. "Come on. If we find Byron, he'll know where it is."

"But where is Byron?" Sheena asked.

"A few Horrors dragged him away," Billy said. "We think they're hiding him somewhere in this theatre."

Matt pointed to a blue door on the rear wall. "That must lead backstage," he said.

He started to jog towards the door. Then he stopped and turned to Sabrina and me. "Come with us. Hurry!" he called.

I shook my head. These kids were creeping me out. I didn't want to join their game. I shivered as a brief image of the Haunted Mask flickered in my mind.

"Sabrina and I just got here," I said. "I think we want to check out some rides instead."

Sabrina frowned at me. "Carly Beth, what's your problem? These guys are totally *cute*," she whispered.

"Didn't we have enough scares back home?" I whispered back.

Matt stepped to the edge of the stage and gazed down at us. "You're special guests, right? Like us?"

"Right," Sabrina said.

"Well, Byron warned us we're *all* in danger," Matt said. "That means you, too."

"Come on," Sabrina said. She dragged me onstage.

We followed the others through the stage door. It led to a long, dark hall with cobwebs clinging to the walls. Our shoes echoed loudly on the concrete floor as we hurried down the hall.

We came to the end and saw two rooms. One room had a gold star on the door. A dressing room. The other door had a sign that read: STORAGE. KEEP OUT.

"Hello? Anyone back here?" Sheena called.

Silence.

121

The dressing room door was open. We peeked inside. No one there. Mondo's black top hat sat on a chair. Jars of make-up were lined up in front of the mirror. His cane leaned against one wall.

"Let's check out the storage room," Sheena said. She pulled open the door, a dim overhead light switched on, and we jammed ourselves inside.

A fluttering sound made me jump. "Someone is here!"

Matt pointed to the wire cages under a small window. "Mondo's pigeons," he said.

Other magic props were stuffed into a tall bookshelf that reached from the floor to the ceiling. Plastic eggs and rubber chickens and fake flowers and wooden bowling pins and white gloves and decks of cards and red-and-blue handkerchiefs. A skull grinned at us from the top shelf.

Mondo's tuxedo jacket hung on a wooden coat rack. I could see a fake bouquet of flowers poking out of one sleeve.

"Byron?" Matt called. "Are you here?"

"We're wasting our time," Billy said. "Come on. Let's go."

We turned and started to the door.

"Wait! Stop!" I cried.

Something on the floor in front of the bookshelf caught my eye. I bent and picked it up. It was a brass name tag. I held it so everyone could see it.

The name engraved on the tag was BYRON.

4

Matt took the name tag from my hand and studied it. "Byron was here," he said.

"Maybe he left it for us to find," Billy said. "He wants us to find him and rescue him."

"But where do we go next?" Sheena asked.

The pigeons fluttered in their cages. They started to warble and coo. Like they were excited, too.

"Wait. There's something else," I said. I reached down to the bottom shelf, where a folded sheet of paper stuck out.

"Be careful," Sabrina said. "It looks very old."

The paper was yellow and stained. It crinkled as I unfolded it. "It must be from an old park guide," I said. "Look." I held it up carefully.

"I don't believe it!" Matt cried. "Check it out!"

The page showed a drawing of a white carousel. Red and orange flames shot off the carousel horses.

"It's the same carousel!" Sheena cried. "The one I saw Britney and Molly riding!"

"But it looks really old," Billy said.

I studied the drawing. "There's a sign next to the carousel," I said. "The page is torn, but I think I can read it."

I read the sign to them: "'Ride the Wheel of Fire! It's Smokin' Hot!'"

"I bet Byron left this for us, too," Matt said. "He wants us to find this ride. He knows that Britney and Molly are there."

"It should be easy enough to find," Sabrina said.

"Let's go. Those girls may be in real danger," Sheena said. She pushed past us and strode back into the hall.

Matt took the old drawing from me. Then he and Billy followed Sheena.

I had no choice. I followed them out of the Haunted Theatre and into the bright sunlight.

The park was crowded. We had to duck and dodge and push our way through Zombie Plaza. I bumped right into a purple-faced Horror with a big metal box strapped to his chest.

He staggered back as I bounced off him. Then he opened the box and pulled out something that looked like a hot dog. "Free Monster Dogs!" he shouted. "Free Monster Dogs! Only one dollar!"

He squinted at me. He had one brown eye and one black eye. "Got a dollar, miss? I'll give you a free Monster Dog for a buck."

I stared at the lumpy brown meat inside the bun. "What's in a Monster Dog?" I asked.

"If you're a dog lover, you don't want to know," he said.

I think he was joking. I didn't want to find out. The others were far ahead of me. I saw Sabrina hurrying to keep up with Matt.

I ducked past a booth with a sign that read NOSE TATTOOS across the front. A Horror leaned on the counter, holding up a long tattoo needle. He had a blue spider tattoo spread over his nose. A smaller sign read: EYEBALLS PIERCED. WHILE-YOU-WAIT.

That made me laugh. I knew it! Everything here was a big joke! Why was Sabrina forcing me to join these kids on their crazy mission?

When I caught up to them, they were studying a big sign. I quickly saw that it was a park directory.

"Over here," Matt said, pointing. "It lists all the HorrorLand rides."

My eyes scanned the long list. Some of the rides caught my eye: The Doom Slide . . . The Bottomless Canoe Ride . . . The Free-fall Bungee Ride. . .

Matt shook his head unhappily. "No Wheel of Fire," he muttered.

"It *has* to be here," Sheena said. "I *saw* it!" She started at the top of the list and began reading them out loud.

"Maybe it's a *new* ride," Billy said. "They're always opening and closing attractions here. Maybe they closed this one a long time ago and just reopened it."

"He's right," Sheena agreed. "Let's search the carnival area." She pointed. "I think it's that way. Across from Goodbye Land."

They started back through the crowd in Zombie Plaza. I pulled Sabrina aside. "Are you sure you want to do this?" I asked.

"Well . . . yeah," Sabrina replied. "Carly Beth, what is your problem? How come you keep wanting to leave? And why did you lie to them? Why didn't you tell them you had a very scary experience, too?"

I shrugged. "I just don't trust them," I said. "You can't trust anyone at HorrorLand. Or any thing. I didn't come here to solve a big mystery about missing girls. I came here to laugh and have fun, Sabrina. And to forget. . ."

Sabrina turned away. "Where are they? We're going to lose them in the crowd."

I started to reply – but my breath caught in my throat.

I shielded my eyes from the bright sunlight and stared at the shop across the plaza from us. The shop was called MAKE A FACE! A mask store.

I gazed into the window and saw a dozen green ugly masks hanging there.

And in the middle of them . . . staring out at me . . . staring out at *me alone* – I saw THE HAUNTED MASK!

5

"No!" I cried out. I grabbed Sabrina's arm.

She let out a squeal. I guess I grabbed her too hard.

I loosened my grip on her arm. "Sabrina – look!" I choked out.

She saw it, too. "Carly Beth, what's the big deal?" she asked. She tugged me towards the little shop.

I pulled back. I wanted to be finished with the Haunted Mask. How could it have followed me to HorrorLand?

The bright sunlight nearly blinded me. I raised a hand to shield my eyes again. The shop window came into focus.

And I saw that it *wasn't* the Haunted Mask. Just another scary green mask with its mouth wide open in a silent scream.

"I . . . I thought. . ." I started. But my mouth was suddenly too dry to talk.

Sabrina rolled her eyes. "I *know* what you thought," she said. "You thought it was the Haunted Mask. But you've got to calm down, Carly Beth. The mask is buried deep outside the stable at Tumbledown Farms."

I nodded. "Yes. I know. But . . . come on. I've just got to take a look inside. I've got to be sure."

My chest felt all fluttery. But I forced myself to walk up to the shop.

We stepped inside. It was a small shop. The walls and shelves were covered with ugly masks.

A Horror stepped out from behind the counter to greet us. She had long black hair tied behind her head in a ponytail, and pale yellow eyes. The curled horns on top of her hair were tinted pink.

"Hi, girls," she said. "Can I sell you a mask today?"

"We're just looking," Sabrina said.

The Horror pulled a hairy wolf mask off the wall and held it out. "You might like this one, Carly Beth," she said.

I gasped. "You know my name?"

She nodded. "You're a very special guest, right?"

Something about the way she said that gave me a chill.

"Try these on," the Horror said. She handed masks to Sabrina and me. "They just came in.

Kind of funny, don't you think? Know what they are? Vampire mice! See the fangs?"

I didn't really want to put the mask on. But the Horror was watching us so intently. I tugged it down over my head.

Yuck. It felt warm inside, like human skin. And the mouse fur on the outside felt totally real. My heart started to pound.

I pulled it off quickly and handed it back to the shopkeeper. Then I helped Sabrina remove hers.

"Cool mask," Sabrina said. She rubbed her hand over a mask that looked like a crying baby. "This totally feels like baby skin," Sabrina said. "How do you make them so real?"

The Horror smiled. "That's a big secret."

All of the ugly faces on the wall were starting to freak me out. "Sabrina, I think we should go," I said.

I started to turn away – then stopped. Something in the back room caught my eye.

"Yes. Go check out the back room," the Horror said. "Lots more interesting masks back there."

Sabrina and I stepped into the tiny room. The wall was covered with masks. They weren't monster masks or animal faces. They all looked like kids.

"How creepy is this?" Sabrina murmured.

I didn't answer. I was staring at two masks near the top.

My hands gripped the counter. My chest felt fluttery again.

"Sabrina – up there," I whispered.

She saw the masks I was staring at. "The two girls," she murmured.

"Yes," I said. "Those masks look just like Britney and Molly. The two missing girls we saw in that little piece of mirror."

"But . . . that's *impossible*," Sabrina said.

Sabrina and I stood there, pressed close together, gazing up at the masks of the two girls.

And as we stared, the girls' lips quivered. The lips on the masks moved up and down.

And they both formed the silent words: *"You're next. . . You're next. . ."*

I couldn't help it. I let out a scream.

"What's wrong?" The shopkeeper appeared behind us.

I pointed to the two masks. "Their lips. . ." I said. "They moved. The masks talked!"

The Horror shook her head. "It only looks that way," she said. "See? The window is open. The wind from the window makes the lips bob up and down."

My mind whirred. I knew she was wrong. The masks were talking to us. Warning us.

The masks appeared to stare down at us. Now their mouths hung open in ugly scowls.

"Those masks look just like two girls we saw," Sabrina said.

"That's funny," the Horror said. "Two girls came in here earlier this week. They said the masks looked like them. But I didn't really think so. Want to try them on?"

131

I shuddered. "Uh . . . no. No thanks," I stammered. I grabbed Sabrina. "Let's go."

We rushed past the Horror, through the front room of the store, and out to the street.

"Come back soon, Carly Beth and Sabrina!" the Horror shouted.

Again, I felt a chill. How did she know our names?

Sabrina and I jogged across the plaza. I had to get away from that mask store. We hurried past several shops.

We stopped in front of a big poster. It showed kids on a beach, sinking deep into the sand. They were screaming and laughing. At the bottom it read: QUICKSAND BEACH. DROP IN ANY TIME!

"We have to find those kids," Sabrina said. "We have to tell them what the masks said. We have to warn them."

I gazed around the plaza. Groups of kids and families were rushing in all directions. They all seemed to be having fun.

I sighed. "Sabrina, maybe we should just find my parents and go home," I said. "Maybe—"

I stopped when I heard voices. Coming from the other side of the big poster.

I poked my head around. Two Horrors leaned against the other side. They were both licking large *black* ice cream cones. *Black* ice cream?!

One of them was huge, tall and bulging with muscles. He wore a red bandanna on his head, tucked around his horns. His friend was skinny and had purple freckles all over his green face.

"Our special guests are in for a lot of heavy-duty surprises – aren't they, Marcus?" the bigger one said.

I ducked my head back out of sight. Was he talking about *us*?

Sabrina started to say something. But I shushed her by pressing my hand over her mouth. We both listened.

"Yeah, Bubba," the smaller one replied. "They don't know how scary things can get."

"Things are gonna get a lot scarier, Marcus," Bubba said. "A *lot* scarier."

"Two are already gone," Marcus said. "We'll take care of the rest."

"We have no choice – do we?"

Sabrina and I froze. My heart pounded. I pressed my back against the poster. We didn't move until the two Horrors walked away.

"Th-they were talking about *us*," I stammered. "Did you hear what they said?"

Sabrina swallowed. "Every word."

"We *do* have to warn the other kids," I said. "You were right, Sabrina. They have to know. Those two Horrors want us ALL to disappear!"

7

We started back towards the Stagger Inn. We thought maybe the kids had returned to the hotel.

The frightening words of the two Horrors kept repeating in my mind:

Two are already gone. . . We'll take care of the rest.

Why did someone want to hurt us or make us disappear? What had they done to Britney and Molly? Why were we invited here?

I had so many questions. My head felt ready to explode!

"Carly Beth, I think we got turned around," Sabrina said. "I think the hotel is back there." She pointed.

I saw small yellow-and-brown cottages up ahead of us. To one side of them, a forest of tall trees. A sign on a wooden pole read: WELCOME TO WEREWOLF VILLAGE. A smaller sign read: CURB YOUR WOLF.

I let out a cry. "Sabrina – look! Is that Billy, Sheena and Matt? Going into the village?"

We took off running. A narrow brick path led into the village. The cottage windows were all dark. The tall trees spread a thick shade over everything. I heard wolf howls up ahead.

Sabrina and I stopped. No sign of the kids. Did I imagine them?

The cottages ended at the forest. We entered the thick grove. Nothing moved. The trees stood perfectly still. We walked and walked in total silence. Then, suddenly, wolf howls rose up all around us.

And two big white wolves stepped on to the path. Their mouths were open. Their tongues hung out over their jagged teeth.

"Oh, no," I murmured. I took a step back.

The wolves lowered their heads. They stared at us with cold grey eyes. Hoarse growls escaped their throats.

"I . . . I don't think they're friendly," I whispered.

The wolves took a step closer, walking side by side. They didn't blink. They kept their cold stares on us as they advanced.

"They can't be real," Sabrina whispered, grabbing my hand. "They wouldn't let real wolves walk around free – would they?"

I didn't answer. The wolves looked ready to pounce.

I cried out when I felt a hand on my shoulder. I spun around to see a smiling Horror. "Don't worry, girls," she said. "They don't bite till after dark."

She made a shooing motion with one hand. The wolves turned and trotted into the woods.

The Horror trotted after them. "Enjoy Wolfsbane Forest!" she called.

"Wait—" I shouted. "How do we get out of here?"

I could hear her footsteps crackling on the blanket of leaves beneath the trees. But she didn't answer.

"I don't see the kids," Sabrina said, brushing a green caterpillar from her hair. "I don't see *any* kids. Let's get out of here."

"I think we came in this way," I said, pointing. The sun had lowered. Long shadows stretched over the forest floor. Hard to see where we were going.

We walked for a while in silence. Caterpillars fell from the trees. I pulled a sticky one off my forehead. I saw two more on Sabrina's shoulder and another one in her hair.

"*Aaaiii!*" I cried out when I felt one drop down the back of my shirt.

"We should have found the path by now," Sabrina said. "Don't tell me we're lost in this awful forest."

"Wait. Are those cottages?" I said. "We must be close to the exit."

We followed a narrow dirt track out of the trees. I was wrong. They weren't cottages. They were large metal cages with bars across the front.

I heard grunts and groans from inside the cages.

Sabrina and I timidly stepped closer. "It's . . . men!" Sabrina whispered.

In the dim grey light, I could see men hunched inside the cages. Some of them gripped the bars with both hands and grunted at us.

The men wore baggy brown shorts. No shirts or shoes. They were covered in bristly black hair. Their chests and backs . . . arms and legs . . . even their feet had thick tufts of hair.

"Actors," Sabrina whispered. "They must work for the park."

I wasn't so sure.

What was real here in HorrorLand? What could you believe and what was make-believe?

One of the men tossed back his long mane of hair and began to howl like a wolf. The others began to bang the bars of their cages with their fists.

I cupped my hands around my mouth and shouted, "Can you help us? We can't find the exit."

They howled and pounded. One of the men hunched on all fours and began to drool.

A man jumped to his feet in the closest cage. He brought his face to the bars. And I saw that he had a *wolf snout* – not a human nose.

I screamed.

He tossed back his head and laughed, a wild-creature laugh.

The horrible laugh sent chills down my back.

"Let's go," Sabrina said, pulling me with both hands. "They are totally creeping me out."

We turned away from the howling, grunting men in their cages. I glanced up at the darkening sky. A pale full moon was rising above the trees.

"This way," I said. I pulled Sabrina towards another dirt track.

I don't know how long we walked through the forest. It seemed like hours.

We both shouted for help as we followed the trail. But no one answered.

"This can't be happening," Sabrina muttered. She pulled another caterpillar off her cheek. "This park is supposed to be FUN!"

"Sabrina – look!" I cried. At the end of the path, I saw a tall wire fence.

I pulled her towards it. "We're out of the forest. Look – a gate!"

My heart thudded in my chest. I wiped sweat off my forehead with the back of my hand. An exit gate! I was so happy.

We raced over the earth. Sabrina got there first. She pushed at the gate. Pushed harder. Tried to pull it open.

That's when I saw the lock. A long silvery padlock.

"It's locked," I said, sighing. My knees suddenly felt weak. "We . . . we're locked in."

With a burst of anger, I grabbed the gate with both hands and shook it. But, of course, it didn't budge.

"*Aaaaagh!*" I uttered a disgusted cry and spun away.

The full moon was bright yellow now. Wolf howls floated in the air all around us.

"We've got to find another exit," Sabrina said. She couldn't keep her voice from trembling. "The wolves really sound hungry. I . . . I think they're *real*! We . . . can't spend the night here."

"We'll follow the fence," I said. "It should lead us out. I—"

I heard scrambling footsteps. Leaves scraping and crackling. The steps came closer.

And then Sabrina and I both screamed in horror as a dark creature leaped out of the trees and fell on us with a hungry cry.

To be continued in . . .

5 DR MANIAC VS ROBBY SCHWARTZ

About the Author

R.L. Stine's books are read all over the world. So far, his books have sold more than 300 million copies, making him one of the most popular children's authors in history. Besides Goosebumps, R.L. Stine has written the teen series Fear Street and the funny series Rotten School, as well as the Mostly Ghostly series, The Nightmare Room series, and the two-book thriller *Dangerous Girls*. R.L. Stine lives in New York with his wife, Jane, and Minnie, his King Charles spaniel. You can learn more about him at www.RLStine.com.

NOW PLAYING IN
HORRORLAND !!!??

THE
HAUNTED THEATRE

Get ready for another year full of SPIRITED events and GLOWING reviews!

Please—No BOO-ing in the auditorium!

OCTOBER 31:
Annual Pumpkin Food Festival

The year begins on Halloween! Join us at midnight for pumpkin-flesh brownies, pumpkin-seed soup, and pumpkin drops. How do you make a pumpkin drop? Toss it off the roof!

NOVEMBER 9–16:
The Dance of the Invisible Spiders

You've never seen one hundred spiders dance like this before. And you never will!

NOVEMBER 27:
All-You-Can-Eat Turkey Dinner

Let our turkeys eat all they can — or you might get GOBBLED.

FIND THE REST at
WWW.ESCAPEHorrorLAND.COM
SIGNED,
LM1

PETS

MAP
#4

Connects to Map #1

They'rrrre Baaaack!

The Original
Bone-Chilling Series fr

FRIGHT-MASTER
R.L. STINE

Now with All-New
Behind-the-Screams
Author Interviews and M

THIS BOOK IS YOUR TICKET TO

www.EnterHorrorLand.com

CHECKLIST #4

- ☐ Creatures have escaped the pet shop. Save Zombie Plaza from a PET-rifying fate!

- ☐ Make your own mask at the MAKE A FACE! mask shop.

- ☐ It's a mask attack! Can you defeat them all?

- ☐ Beware of a sonic nightmare at the Haunted Theatre. FACE off against the Haunted Mask before you turn into a monster – for ever!

USER NAME

PASSWORD

NOW WITH BONUS FEATURES!